GW00492582

CHILDREN OF THE WISE OAK

All the best

CHILDREN OF THE WISE OAK

WISE OAK SERIES BOOK 1

OLIVER J TOOLEY

Blue poppy publishing

Published by Blue Poppy Publishing Devon
EX34 9HG info@bluepoppypublishing.co.uk
Edited by Sarah Dawes – Bishop's Nympton, Devon
Cover art Iver Klingenberg – Porlock, Somerset
Cover design Andy Jones – Bishop's Nympton, Devon
Printed by Short Run Press – Exeter, Devon

1ˢᵗ Edition Hardcover ISBN-13: 978-1-911438-00-7
1ˢᵗ Edition Paperback ISBN-13: 978-1-911438-01-4

To Morton, Kai, and Ashdon,
who started this whole crazy thing off.

THANKS ARE OWED TO:

www.latinforum.org - for various Latin translations.

Sarah Dawes - for editing, and proofreading.

Iver Klingenberg – for the front cover artwork

Andy Jones – for the overall cover design

Teachers – all teachers, not just the ones who struggled to get me to learn anything.

Fiction authors including, but not limited to: J.K.Rowling, Caroline Lawrence, Michelle Paver and Terry Pratchett – for inspiration and, in the case of Caroline, actual encouragement and advice.

Non-fiction authors including, but not limited to: Francis Pryor, Barry Cunliffe, Thomas Rolleston, Eckart Köhne & Cornelia Ewigleben and others – for information.

www.unrv.com - for all sorts of help with historical facts about the Roman empire.

Innumerable other internet sources of information about everything from Celtic religion to the dates of solar eclipses.

New Barn Celtic village in Dorset, which is the physical location of Ba-Dun in the story. My son went there on a week-long school trip and came back with so many tales about Celtic life. He also showed me how to make butter, among other things.

Butser Ancient Farm for more advice.

This book could never have been printed without the financial backing of the following people.

Sarah and Simon Thompson

who bought the cover painting.

David Tubby whose support has been overwhelming, but most welcome.

Morton Tooley, Craig Halls, and Graham Stuttaford.

Phillip Dutton, Thomas J. Arnold, Mac & Carole McGill, and Mark Medcalf

James and Erin Rasile, Virginia Clark, Jean-Luc Crisanto G. Reyes, Bridget Evangeline Gray, Ann Cavanagh, Stef Wischhusen, Naomi Galvin, Sarah Gallagher, Ingrid Guy, Phil Halliwell, Roger Short, Pleione Tooley, Steve Jones, Mike Thomas, Sarah Dawes, Wayne Green, Netti & Frank Pearson, Tony Dredster, Mike Lee, ♥Mary Brennan♥, ♥Luca Ray Nolan♥

Lindsay Wilson, Jonathan, Yael, Emily & Daniel Dital, Brad Bunyard, Sean Keating, Jim Jones, Jane Armstrong, Stephen Shelton, Wilton Catford, Jez Evans, Paul Gates, Patricia Bagshaw, Victoria Collins, Cathy Edwards, Sue Curtis, Matt Chammings, Pam Thomas, Barry Booth, Ms. Yvonne Hin, Yazzy, David Hancock, Tracey Casburn, Sammy Azzopardi-Slinn, Johnny Morocco, Marting Wilson, Joe Silver, Jim Thurston, Ruth Downie, Dawn Connor-Van Der Horst, Sam Gilbert, Jason Cross Magdaléna Kacejová

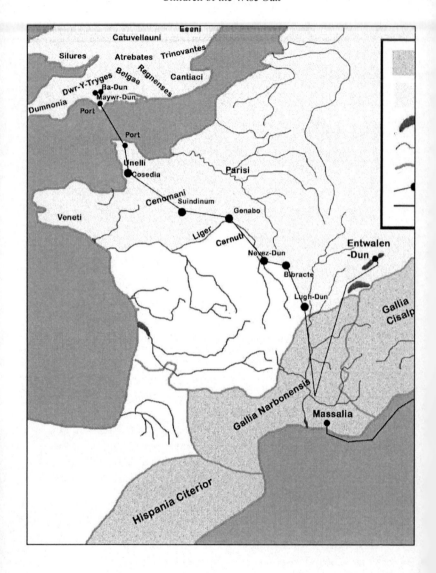

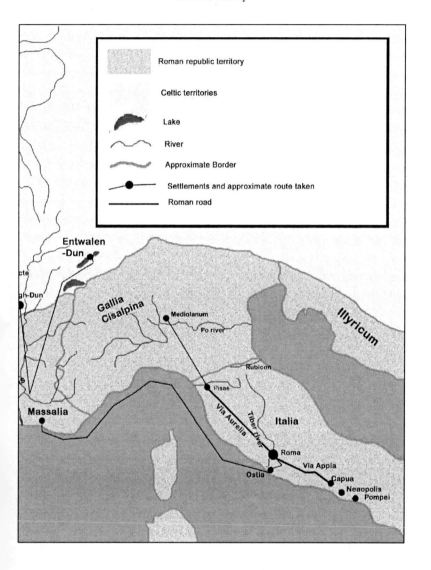

1

It was a cold morning just before Imbolc. The sky faded gradually from the deep translucent blue of twilight to the pale milky blue of pre-dawn, as the god Bellenos began his daily journey across the heavens. His burning chariot emerged proudly on the horizon, behind low rolling hills dusted with white; at first blinding, making the foreground appear darker. Then the intense light of the sun-god rose higher, spreading his warmth, igniting frozen dewdrops on innumerable blades of grass, and transforming every tiny crystal of frost on the branches of trees into microscopic rainbows.

Teague woke early as usual and stretched slowly, then shivered as it was bitterly cold. He woke the sleeping fire and fed it some more wood before pulling on his shoes and cloak and going outside. He walked down to the well for water, which he brought back and set to warm over the fire. He was always first up and always fastest to sleep. He often drifted off during the day if not too much was happening.

The activity disturbed his brothers, Blyth and Abbon, who stirred and rubbed their eyes wearily. Blyth was the oldest; at nearly fourteen he was practically a man. Slim and muscular, he was strong, and yet disliked fighting and did not look forward to warrior training. Abbon was the youngest, at ten. He was cheeky and irrepressible. He loved to run around and tease his older brothers, then dodge out of the way of their blows.

The three dressed and left before their mother even woke, knowing that she was tired from caring for their little sister. Elarch was often ill; she had a pale complexion and platinum blonde hair that framed a porcelain face with china blue eyes. Slim and graceful with a long neck and high cheekbones, she lay curled up on her mother's furs, fast asleep, as the boys left the house.

Today they would have to go and collect as much firewood as possible for the great feast of Imbolc. This was an important festival marking the end of winter. Fires would be lit, sacrifices made, and prophesies for the coming year would be sought. Everything from the weather and the crops, to new life and death might be foretold.

The three ventured out of the camp, through the gates in the tall wooden fence, decorated with the skulls of enemies slain in battle, weaving through the slopes and ditches that made up the defences against attack, and down the hill to the edge of the woods. Things had been pretty peaceful lately; the Gods had been kind, and the seasons mild, providing plentiful food for animals and people alike. The rivers were full, fish jumping, and there was plenty of trade both far and near. As a result the defences were in poor repair, with stakes not driven deep into the soil and the ridges crumbling to fill the ditches in places. The woods were never quite safe though, as wild animals always lurked and, it was said, there was a huge beast that carried away unwary children, never to be seen again.

"Don't you go falling asleep now Teague!" called Blyth.

"As if," grumbled Teague. He was only too well aware of the dangers of the forest. He was perhaps the most timid of the three. He had a gentle artistic nature, which his mother saw, but his uncle, Kyndyrn, could not accept. Not that he was a coward; he would just try to avoid a fight until there was nowhere left to go. When he was cornered he would turn, and cold fury took over. His uncle had done it once, goading him to fight; he had pushed Teague over the edge until, with no way to back out gracefully, the boy's eyes seemed to glaze over and his muscles tensed. He had leaped with unexpected force and speed, knocking Kyndyrn over and scratching at his face. As a result Kyndyrn, the strongest warrior in the clan, had red scratches down both cheeks for several days. Teague's mother had intervened to stop him being punished.

"You got what you wanted little brother, you made him fight, now leave him be!" she said, as her eyes burned into him.

While Kyndyrn was a fierce warrior, he knew his sister Epona was a powerful mage. Her curse had been known to kill a man, so he let it drop.

In the woods there were plenty of fallen branches from the strong winds of the previous night and collecting was good. The boys loaded up wheeled carts as they went, but soon, as the weak sun reached its highest point in the grey sky, Abbon's thoughts turned to mischief. He found a few old acorns that had fallen on barren soil and decided on some target practice. Choosing his aim carefully, and from a good distance, he hit Blyth hard on the back of the head, then carried on collecting as if nothing had happened. Blyth turned angrily to see the source of this small missile, at first blaming Teague who was completely innocent, and said as much. A few minutes later Teague was struck on the side of the face and there was no doubt where the shot had come from.

"Cut it out Abbon! We have work to do!"

"What?" said Abbon, with his best innocent look on his face.

Blyth gave Abbon a glare that said, 'try that one more time and it will be the last thing you do'.

Abbon let it go until all was forgotten and then let loose a couple of quick shots, one at each brother. The two older siblings dropped everything and gave chase but Abbon was already running and, with a fair head start, he leaped into the branches of a tree. He was a very good climber, showing absolutely no fear. His long slender fingers caught hold of the thinnest branches that would support his weight and he clambered out of sight into clumps of ivy strangling an old oak.

"Get down from there NOW!" shouted Blyth, with little hope of obedience.

"Come on Abbon, we won't do anything," said Teague, somewhat untruthfully.

Abbon inched out along a branch and across to another tree. Leaf buds were poking through here and there; ivy gave some cover. With dense undergrowth of ferns and holly, Abbon hoped he could avoid being seen. He headed deeper into the woods where he could avoid coming down, hoping to get away long enough for them to cool down, but his brothers followed the sounds of creaking branches relentlessly.

It was decidedly cooler and darker here. There was a sense in the air of foreboding. Even Abbon realised they were too far into the forest, and fear of the unknown began to overtake fear of his brothers. Likewise his brothers were more worried about beasts, both real and mythical, than getting revenge on their little brother.

"Abbon! Come on, stop messing around, we have to get back!" called Blyth.

No sound came. Blyth and Teague had lost track of

Abbon completely. Then a little voice came from just above their heads.

"I'm scared."

"Me too," admitted Teague. "Come down and let's get out of here."

Abbon dropped to the ground right in front of Blyth.

"You idiot Abbon, we'll be late back now. Come on, it's this way I think."

After giving Abbon a half-hearted clip round the ear, Blyth led the way back as best he could remember. There was a path of sorts, which was probably a regular track for deer and boar, and he followed that for some way before striking out across a large patch of ferns which they had damaged on their way through earlier.

Soon, however, it became clear that he was lost again. There was nothing familiar but Blyth kept on going, not wanting to admit the truth. Teague knew it wasn't right but would not say anything for fear of getting shouted at. After what seemed like hours, but may only have been minutes, they noticed a smell of smoke. There was a huge ancient oak, with a crown of nine boughs that split from the trunk several feet above the ground. The gnarled and misshapen bark below the crown resembled a face, with a dark and gaping maw. It looked like a particularly fierce and malevolent warrior. A little further ahead they saw what looked like a clearing and some sort of fire. A huge conical pile of moss and earth stood seething with grey smoke before a small round hut. Blyth called out to see if there was anyone inside.

A small man appeared in the doorway. He looked ancient yet sprightly; deep wrinkles covered every corner of his animated clean-shaven face, his eyes twinkled and his mouth flickered into a smile of sorts, tinged with sadness. He dressed in an uncommon manner, with shoes that were clearly not obtained locally. His cloak was linen and a rich deep purple, hemmed with gold.

"Why do you come here?" he asked in a quiet, hoarse voice.

"We... got lost," said Blyth, feeling strangely afraid.

Something about the man and the place unnerved him. Teague and Abbon felt it too. They were silent, and stood well back from the hut.

"You are from Ba-Dun," the old man said. It was a statement, not a question. Perhaps this was obvious as it was the nearest settlement.

"The children of Trethiwr."

How did he know? Blyth must have looked surprised, because he added, "You are the image of your father, boy. How is he?"

"We have not seen him since just after our sister Elarch was born. Uncle says he is probably dead." Blyth spoke with only a tinge of sadness; he had seen his father so rarely in the last thirteen years, although he remembered hearing his stories of far-off lands, of different tribes and cultures, and of strange dialects and languages.

"He is not dead," stated the man, without any doubt in his voice. "It is a time for prophesy, so I will tell you this. Your father will return soon. Go now, that way, as quickly as possible. A storm is coming and you need to get back to the fort."

Blyth wanted to ask questions but as he took a breath the man said again, "Go NOW!" He pointed again in the direction they should head and his expression left no invitation for further discussion.

The fire grew hotter and glowed red, issuing spurts of billowing smoke. The boys were filled with an overwhelming sense of dread. They ran, and even as they turned to look back, the hut, the man and the fire were nowhere to be seen. Blyth led the way again as they crashed through overhanging branches and low scrub until the trees thinned and they found themselves at the edge of the forest once more, not far from their carts.

It was already darkening as the weak sun held on to the horizon with thin fingers, before dropping out of sight. They threw a few more stray sticks on the carts, tied their loads down, and raced back to the village as fast as their burdens would allow. Blyth had to go back several times to help Abbon, who kept getting stuck and once overturned his load. They arrived back cold, yet sweaty, to find the whole village a buzz of frenetic activity. Kyndyrn stopped only long enough to hit them all, and shout about how late they were. Their wood was thrown onto a huge, already burning, pyre and they headed off to join in the celebrations.

There was no sign of a storm, however. "Perhaps," thought Blyth, "the old man is not a seer but just a crazy old man." But the way he had disappeared, along with the house, and the fire, was still very mysterious. Anyway, it would have to wait until after the feast.

2

Everyone in the clan was there, gathered in the central clearing surrounded by Chief Urien's hut, the smithy, store hut, granary, meeting house, and the temple. Set back from here was the house of Urien's advisor, Darruwen the Mage, who was probably the most powerful man in the village.

Blyth's cousin Blodwyth was dressed all in white and holding a torch in one hand and a staff of white aspen, wound around with holly and mistletoe, in the other, to represent Brigantia, Goddess of fire and smith craft, bringer of spring, Goddess of healing, and of poetry. She looked more beautiful than ever and feelings stirred in Blyth, feelings of unexplained aching, tingling, making the hairs on his neck stand up and making him feel both weak and strong at the same time.

Rodokoun was there also; a young and fierce warrior, a few years older than Blyth, who divided his time between practicing with sword or spear, and following Blodwyth around trying to attract her attention, running his fingers through his long red hair. Blyth did not like him but kept out of his way to avoid a fight which he knew he would lose.

Blodwyth was seated on a chariot, pulled by two oxen and held fast to trees on either side by long white ropes of flax, to represent Brigantia's winter prison of ice. The oxen were nervous and stamping agitatedly as the fire burned fiercely only twenty or so paces away. There were many villagers with burning torches on all sides. At a signal from the Mage, some of them held the torches to the flax ropes which burned and released the chariot, freeing Brigantia who rode forth bringing spring to the world. Blodwyth handed out sprigs of evergreen branches to the people as she passed. Then Blodwyth was required to wield a large sacrificial knife made of flint, supposedly wrought by Deus Pater himself, but perhaps more likely by a member of the tribe now long dead. Nevertheless it was very old and was kept safe, when not in use, by the Mage, in a secret place in his hut.

Blodwyth was brought a calf, born last year. She had seen it take its first steps. Now she cut swiftly and surely across its throat and watched the blood spurt from its neck as it was taken away. Next a lamb, of similar age, and lastly a chicken. Each was killed in the same

11

manner, and carried away. A portion would be burned as an offering to the Deities. The Mage would examine the entrails and carry out rituals to divine prophesies for the coming year. Lastly the remainder would be butchered for future meals.

Food was now distributed which had already been cooked at hearths around the village. Roast boar, mutton, beef, and chicken, root vegetables, and bread made from barley and wheat, herbs and pulses. To drink there was beer and mead, and for the Chief and important people there was also wine from across the sea. All the village ate well this day, although they had suffered shortages recently, and there would be more before the spring really took over from winter. The grain store was now empty, game was scarce, and the ground was still hard and barren. Ewes were beginning to produce milk and some of this would be used to make butter, a vital source of fat. A warm start to spring would help, of course.

The bard played the harp and sang songs telling old stories of Brigantia, and of Deus Pater, the sky father, Chief God from whom all the Keltoi were supposedly descended; of Cernunnos, the horned God; and of Lugh, God of light, skilled in all arts, messenger, and God of merchants.

Towards the end of the feast, Darruwen stepped up to a raised platform and called for quiet. Torches mounted on either side lit his red beard and hair in the darkness and his black eyes reflected the dancing light like dying stars in a moonless sky. As the village fell silent he announced, "I have divined the weather for the coming season, and the omens are good. Brigantia smiles upon us all once more and the season will be mild, providing us with good crops and plenty of game!"

A roar of approval went up from the throng, and they fell to drunken chattering about their plans for the coming year; what crops they would plant where, and what hunting trips they would make.

Darruwen, however, cleared his throat and the hubbub subdued again.

"However, there will come among us one who has deserted us, and now returns with false prophesies of war and destruction."

He then stood down without further comment, returning to his hut, and left the rest to supposition and rumour.

"Who has deserted us and why would they return?" was the question on everyone's lips.

The drink continued to flow and the prophesy was forgotten amid drunken arguments about past hunting glories, and who had the last of the boar. At one point two young warriors, Gerwain and Rodovour, who had been arguing for some time, jumped up, their swords drawn. They were cousins, and normally great friends, but too much beer and wine had made them foolish and impetuous. They squared up to each other and after a few wild drunken slashes Gerwain drew first blood and now Rodovour, like a wounded animal, was slashing and thrusting with wild abandon as his cousin backed away defensively. But now the bard jumped up and made up a song on the spot, mocking the two warriors,

"I tell the tale of brave Gerwain
Who by his friend and kin was slain
And of heroic Rodovour
Who killed his cousin over boar…"

It may not have been great poetry but it soon had the company laughing, and the laughter and the irony got through to the two hotheads who took in the words and stopped fighting.

"Then brave Gerwain first dropped his guard
And Rodovour put down his sword
The cousins held each other long
All thanks to my fantastic song."

Amid gales of laughter and a few friendly slaps on the back the fight was forgotten, with a toast of more ale to cement their friendship again.

Eventually most of the village had drifted away to hearth and home and slept soundly on raised platforms covered in furs. Even the most hardened drinkers slept where they had sat; one with his cup upturned over his reddened face.

The morning was the brightest it had been for the year. It was a day of rest. Those who had slept outdoors woke with the bright rays of the sun burning through their eyelids and retreated to the darkness of their huts to reacquaint themselves with sleep once more. Blyth was up first, unusually for him. He had not slept well. The prophesies of the day before disturbed him. His father would return after six years away and the Mage was predicting a deserter coming amongst them with bad news. Were these two prophesies connected? He needed to speak to his mother first and see if she knew anything. She woke early as well, after the first uninterrupted night's sleep she had enjoyed for some time. Elarch was still sleeping soundly after finding one or two unattended mead cups which she had drained, unnoticed by their owners. A few fights had started over that, but nobody was killed so no harm done.

"I need to talk with you, mother," said Blyth. "Something very strange happened yesterday."

"Let's go for a walk then; I need some fresh air," she replied.

Blyth's mother, Epona, was the daughter of the present Chief's brother. Her mother was the daughter of a great king, from a far-off land across the eastern sea.

Her hair reached her waist. She wore it tied back and it flicked and flashed reddish gold in the bright wintry sunlight as she led the way down a path towards the hazel coppice to the south of the village. She moved lightly; always sure-footed, even on rough ground.

The coppice wood provided the wattle for building hut walls, and sticks for basket weaving. It also provided a windbreak against the worst storms, and now a secluded place for conversation.

"Yesterday in the woods, there was an old man," began Blyth.

His mother said nothing so he continued, "He knew who I was, or rather he knew who my father was, and he told us that he would return soon."

"So he is still alive then," said Epona, her eyes misty and looking off into the middle distance.

"This man said he was," offered Blyth, assuming she was referring to his father, but Epona smiled and said,

"I meant, Kaito, your great grandfather, and my great uncle… the man you met," she added, watching her son for his reaction.

It dawned slowly on Blyth, who had been taken by surprise by this revelation.

"My great-grandfather is still alive?" he asked incredulously. "And living alone in the forest so close by?" he added.

"He chose his path a long time ago," was all his mother said.

Blyth remembered his original question.

"So how does he know father is coming back and what did Darruwen mean about a deserter returning?

"Kaito was… is a powerful Mage. He spent years travelling to far-off lands to learn all he could about magic. When his brother, the old Chief, died and Urien became Chief they didn't get on well. Urien sought the glory and riches of war. Kaito sought riches through trade, and the lasting wealth of peace. Urien seeks to unite people under his rule. Kaito seeks to unite people in a common goal for the good of all. Urien won over the clan and we went to war with neighbouring villages. Now they pay tribute, but grudgingly, and we still pay tribute to Maywr-Dun to the west, so nothing really was achieved; but Urien got some nice heads to mount over the gates, and that at least will ward off any invading enemies. Kaito chose to live alone in the forest and withdraw from the clan. If he says your father will return then he probably will. Kaito is rarely wrong."

"He was wrong about the storm. He said there was a storm coming."

"Did he say when?"

"Well he said we had to go, right away. I assumed he meant last night, and there wasn't."

"Did he say what kind of storm?"

"A storm! How many kinds of storm are there? Snowstorms, thunderstorms, windstorms... !"

Epona let it drop; Blyth could not control his temper and he didn't understand metaphors. She decided it was easier to agree with him.

"Well, perhaps he was wrong about that," she conceded. "Come on, let's head back."

3

The village was stirring when Epona and Blyth returned to their hut. Men and women were going about the morning routine, grimacing with ill-concealed pain at every loud sound, and squinting at the bright sun. In the days to come there would be much work to do. Ploughing fields for sowing barley, rye, wheat, and beans, as well as root vegetables. Cows and ewes would need to be watched closely, as they were heavy with young, and calving would commence soon, followed quickly by the lambs. But today would be a chance for quiet and rest. Judging by the frayed nerves and sore heads of some of the more dedicated followers of Govanno, God of alcohol, rest was probably a good thing.

In the evening many villagers, especially children, gathered in the meeting house for storytelling. Beside the large central fire - mainly willow, with the bark stripped off to reduce smoke - Darruwen told the story of Brynno and how he led his army to victory over the Romani. Children, curled up in mothers' laps or cross-legged on furs, and older folk on log benches, listened in hushed awe to the adventures of the legendary warrior king.

"Some three hundred years ago our ancestors had spread across the known world, south as far as the southern sea, west to the ocean at the edge of the world, and east beyond the great mountains to the eastern sea. The Helleni who lived to the south called all our people Keltoi, although then, as now, there were many different tribes. One of these tribes, the Sennoni, moved into land to the south of the great central mountains, where they were challenged by people called Y-Trwsgani, who had farms there, and a huge fortified town of thousands of people.

"They owed their allegiance to the Romani whose main city, Roma, was further to the south. But the warm southern lands of plentiful food and wine had softened these people and, when Brynno led an army against them, they hid inside their town and fired huge stones from inside their strong stone walls. Brynno laid siege to the town for many days until a small force of Romani arrived to negotiate for peace. But the Roman envoys were not very diplomatic. The negotiations were led by three brothers: Quinto, Caeso, and Numero, of the Fabio family. Instead of begging Brynno for mercy; which he may have given in exchange for gold and land;

their chief negotiator, Marcus, threatened to send an army to drive all the tribes out of 'Roman' lands.

"Brynno laughed out loud at this threat, and asked where this so-called army was. He pretended to search under the table and even caused indignation by lifting the robe of Quinto, to see if perhaps they were hidden under there."

The hut echoed with laughter at this part of the story. When it died down the Mage continued, his smile turning serious once more.

"Everything broke up at that; the three brothers drew swords and retreated, as one, to their guard. They mounted their horses as Brynno and his men laughed even more at the humiliated Romani. They were so doubled up with laughing that they were off their guard, and Quinto threw a spear which hit Chieftain Pretano. Brynno pulled the spear out, but the wound was obviously fatal."

A few sighs and whistles went around the hut. Pretano was said to be the ancestor of all the island tribes hence the name used for the island: Pretan. Darruwen went on in a more urgent tone now, pacing around the fire, his hands animated, the firelight dancing in his eyes, as he set the scene.

"Brynno held his sword in two hands, the point down, and he swore the triple oath:

'I Brynno, king of the Sennoni, swear to avenge my ally and comrade in arms, Pretano; family head of the Pretani. If I fail, may the sky fall down upon me, may the seas rise up and cover me, may the earth open up and swallow me!'"

The silence in the hut was absolute.

"Without further ado, Brynno prepared his armies to pursue the killers, and marched on Rome itself. The Romani had saved their allies, Y-Trwsgani, but not as they intended. Instead of scaring Brynno away they had brought the entire weight of his armies to their doorstep.

"A large vanguard went first and demanded the murderer be handed over along with his accomplices. The Romani refused and even had the audacity to appoint the brothers as Chieftains in Roma. Brynno was not to be put off, nor was he afraid. Despite strong walls and a large and organised army, the Romani are weak compared to us. They hide behind shields and walls. They wear not only clothes but armour which covers their entire bodies leaving no part unprotected. But our swords are charmed with blessings from the Gods and can cut through even the strongest armour."

"It's true!" exclaimed one battle-hardened elder.

"Word spread that Brynno was going to attack Rome, and he met with emissaries from Rome's enemies in the south. He persuaded them that he needed gold to pay for mercenaries. They gave him five hundred pounds of gold, about the weight of a fully-armed warrior. He only engaged enough mercenaries to persuade them that he had spent the money wisely but he kept most of it for himself. Hired swordsmen are no match for our warriors with Toutatis on our side."

More murmurs of agreement filled the meeting house at this statement.

"As they approached Rome an army, led by a general named Quinto-Sulpico, stood in their path. They stood two hundred deep and five hundred across in the main body, with rectangular shields interlocked in front and above, like the shell of a tortoise. Throwing spears made no impact, but just bounced off like raindrops on the leaves of the oak tree."

Darruwen's voice rose and fell, like the waves of the sea, adding excitement to every sentence.

"Then a hundred men and women, wearing nothing but blue paint on their bodies, with lime in their hair, and armed only with the long sword and round shield, went forward. At first, screaming and beating their shields with their swords, they terrified the front lines of the enemy who could see them. They had all consumed a potion of special herbs which inhibit pain and speed the heart. Their eyes were blank yet all-seeing, and they had no concept of fear."

At this the older members of the audience nodded sagely, having seen this potion used. A few had even imbibed it before battle themselves. The Mage continued,

"The weak Romani, all men, could not believe they were about to be attacked by such wild and ferocious warriors. Worse; they have a code of honour which prohibits warfare against women."

Some of the women in the hut tutted their disgust at such an attitude.

"Confusion filled the Romani front ranks, when the warriors charged as one at a single point in the line. The first assault crashed so hard against the shield wall that swords and shields alike broke, and men toppled back against the second and third ranks. The remaining attackers poured into the breach, slashing in every direction at once, with their swords piercing armour like butter. The scent of blood was in their nostrils and a great cry went up from the main ranks of Brynno's army."

His voice was at a crescendo of frenetic energy at this point, the pace of the story matching the speed of the warriors he was describing.

"Chariots rode forwards now, turning tightly at the breach. The drivers loosed spears into the melee, and elite fighters in armour, some even with helmets, joined in the battle. Brynno could be seen in the very centre of the action, his sword flashing back and forth cutting down man after man, his shield loose by his side, inspiring his men and women to greater heroics. Horsemen rode in from the flanks and cut down many stragglers who had broken ranks. Eventually the crushed Romani managed to regroup and retreat. It is said they were protected behind walls of their own dead as they fled the field!

"Brynno regrouped his armies and, after caring for the wounded and arranging the proper rites for the dead, he continued on to Rome itself."

There was a brief pause here; whether it was for Darruwen to catch his breath, or for the listeners, was not clear.

"Here he found women and children, as well as old men, fleeing the city in huge numbers. He allowed them to leave, being a merciful leader as well as a great warrior king. Then he spotted the murderer, Quinto Fabio, among the civilians and he dispatched some of his warriors to deal with him. The coward hid behind weak and unarmed people who were slaughtered by the overeager warriors, but Quinto was at least now dealt with, and Pretano was avenged.

"The armies of Brynno then advanced almost unopposed into Rome, where most of the defenders had gathered in the central area, which was the most heavily fortified. It was larger even than Maywr-Dun, with walls that reached the clouds and gates as thick as a full grown oak tree.

"Brynno ordered treasures to be removed with care, as he was a wise ruler who prized the arts as much as he prized great prowess on the battlefield. Alas, in the heat of the situation, a great many items were damaged and a number of fires were accidentally started by careless soldiers holding torches too high. Or possibly the Romani destroyed their own houses to stop Brynno's armies getting their hands on them. It is ever the case in war that beauty is destroyed in the stampede for victory."

His audience nodded sagely at this.

"The Romani held out for several moons until their food ran short and they were forced to surrender completely. Brynno offered them fair terms; ten hundred pounds of gold, which they eventually accepted. Yet even then, at the weighing, they quibbled about the process, claiming that Brynno was using extra-heavy weights. Brynno was insulted by this accusation and heartily sick and tired of these officious degenerates. As a last punishment for them, he threw his sword onto the scales with the weights. The Romani began to protest once more so he spoke to them in their own tongue saying, 'Vae Victis' - woe to the vanquished.

"Brynno left with his armies and the spoils of war and the Romani were put properly in their place."

As the Mage concluded his story he stood, and muttered a prayer to the Gods. Then he cast some dust onto the fire which burst with a flash of green flame and filled the room with smoke. When the smoke cleared he had disappeared.

Some of the salient facts of his story differed significantly from versions being told to children in Rome and, in fact, the reality was that the Romani had grown much more powerful in the intervening few hundred years. They had expanded into much land which had previously been held by tribes of the Keltoi. They had never forgiven what they saw as the looting and destruction of their capital, the wholesale slaughter of innocent women and children, and the utter humiliation brought upon them by the savages known as the Keltoi and their leader Brennus. The Romani had subjugated their enemies in the south and to the east, and now controlled the great southern sea which they called the Mare Nostrum - 'Our Sea'. Now they were turning their attention to exacting revenge for that defeat of three hundred years earlier. They already controlled all the coastal areas to the north and south around the Mare Nostrum and most of what they called Hispania, the Keltoi land to the west. Some tribes had migrated to Eiru, to escape, while others had accepted Roman rule.

But these facts were easy to ignore in the insular world of the Dwr-Y-Tryges in the south of the island of Pretan.

4

A merchant arrived on the next day with a cart loaded with grain. The tribal Chief at Maywr-Dun, Kano-Walo, had been frugal this year and had managed to retain a small surplus, knowing he could trade food for much more than usual at this time of year.

Urien parted with ten young hunting dogs (to be traded across the sea, perhaps ending up in a Roman town), a horse, and two newly-made shields, fashioned in a unique horn shape rather than the usual oval. He also paid a pound in weight of coins, recognised among the Dwr-Y-Tryges as currency; this was Urien's tribute to his more powerful neighbour. The coins were, supposedly, mainly gold but more and more silver was creeping into them lately; no doubt someone at the mint on the coast was taking a nice profit out for themselves.

The weather continued bright and clear with

freezing cold nights, frosty mornings clearing quickly after sunrise, and giving warm afternoons, out of keeping with the season. Three days after the merchant had visited, a lone traveller was seen on the road coming from Maywr-Dun, walking casually and leading two horses pulling a loaded cart. He looked like another merchant, which he was, of a sort. But he was also Trethiwr, father to Blyth, Teague, Abbon, and Elarch, and life partner to Epona. He was returning, after a six-year absence, with many stories to tell and bad news for the people of Pretan.

As he drew closer some of the older villagers and peasants, out ploughing the fields, recognised him and renewed old acquaintances. Not everyone was welcoming. Darruwen's words began to fit into place for one or two people. They were reluctant to be too friendly until they were sure what the Mage would say. Until the Chief had officially welcomed him back to the clan he was technically an outsider.

Urien waited at the main gate, framed by the skulls of his slain enemies, with Darruwen by his side. The Mage carried a large oak staff topped with a piece of amber as big as a fist. He wore his best blue linen cloak and a large gold torc around his neck as well as many gold arm torcs. This was not in honour of Trethiwr, but to intimidate him. The Chief wore chain-mail as well as a bronze breastplate and leg guards and a full helmet with cheek plates and visor. In his right hand he carried a long spear, and three throwing javelins in his shield hand. The shield was of the horn shape favoured in the region, embossed with bronze and coloured with Urien's personal insignia. His cloak was imported from far away across the sea and was of the finest heavy cotton, tightly woven, and dyed a deep rich blue. He wore his sword and dagger in leather sheaths on his belt. Last but not least he wore a torc, woven in many strands of pure gold, intricately crafted to create a taper from the ends, as thick as a finger, to the middle, as thick as a wrist.

Trethiwr approached the Chief and stood before him. He wore simple clothing obtained in Maywr-Dun, of the most typical local origins. He carried no weapons and no shield and he knelt before the Chief with his head bowed. It was a tense moment. Urien could choose to turn and walk away, whereupon the gates would be shut and Trethiwr would know he was not welcome. He could return to Maywr-Dun and seek service with the Chief there or continue his travels elsewhere, but he would forever be barred from his home village. Alternatively the Chief could simply strike him down where he knelt. This was highly unlikely, as it was usually reserved for known rebels and traitors. Lastly he could offer his hand to welcome Trethiwr back into the clan.

Darruwen had advised Urien strongly, in private, to refuse his return, saying that he was at best a deserter and at worst a possible traitor. Epona had begged Urien to allow her husband to return. A battle raged inside

Urien's head. Both the Mage and Epona were using all their secret powers on him. His own will was subjugated as they fought against each other for their desired outcome. Darruwen focused his silent incantation through his staff, while Epona held her hands inside her cloak, spelling magic words on her fingers.

After what seemed like an age Urien held his hand out to Trethiwr and pulled him to his feet. Trethiwr pulled back his cloak and reached to an amulet hanging from his neck. It was pure gold, about the length and thickness of a thumb, and fashioned in the shape of a cross with a loop at the top.

"This is a symbol of life and brings long life to the wearer. It is a gift for you Chief Urien," said Trethiwr.

They turned and walked together through the gates, followed by Kyndyrn, Darruwen, Epona, and several warriors. Urien led the way to his own hut. Trethiwr followed him inside, along with Darruwen and Epona. The wagon was left in the central clearing and the horses were taken away, to be fed and watered, by stable servants.

In the dark of the Chief's hut, Trethiwr sat by the fire and accepted a drink of mead. Urien was first to break the silence.

"You have given me a gift of great price Trethiwr; now I must reciprocate. I see you have no weapons? As usual. Do you abhor violence so much that you would let any robber steal everything from you without so much as a dagger to protect you?"

"There is more of value than worldly goods," was Trethiwr's quiet reply.

"Even so, you can't go around Ba-Dun like some common servant with no arms."

Urien called for a sword to be brought from the stores. He drew it from the sheath and handed it, hilt first, to Trethiwr, who accepted it and uttered a prayer to Bellenos that it would serve him well. Formalities over, the conversation became more casual.

"Tell us of your adventures, Trethiwr," ordered Urien.

"There is so much to tell. Why don't I start at the end?" he said with a wry smile. "I've just come from Maywr-Dun. Your bargain for their grain arrived just before I left. I recognised the shield; a fine piece of work. Kano-Walo was most pleased. The horse was also well received, as were the dogs... at first." He grinned a wicked grin. "Big fine hunting dogs they will grow into, but still young and half trained as you no doubt know. They were tethered to posts near the village gates, but nobody had the sense to feed them. Then a hunting party arrived back from a successful hunt."

Trethiwr paused for effect before continuing.

"The smell of blood was on the hunters and the dogs caught the scent and started baying and straining at the ropes. Then all of a sudden the stake was pulled out of the ground and the whole pack raced at the hunters, who dropped their prize and ran for their lives. Some of the dogs stopped to investigate the carcass, a huge wild boar. The rest carried on, after the live prey, barking like crazy. The hunters headed for the nearest trees, a stand of alders near the stream. Of course everyone knows alders grow well in bogs and wetlands but in their panic they forgot that. The ground was completely waterlogged and they ran headlong into the marsh. Some of them sank almost to their waists! Luckily for them the dogs had more sense. Having had their sport they left the hunters wallowing in the mire to rejoin the rest of the pack at the feast!"

Roars of laughter filled the hut.

"It was all sorted out in the end, but the dogs had the best of the boar; and the hunters had to walk, dripping wet and filthy with mud, right through the village without their kill!"

Trethiwr, seemingly, had an inexhaustible supply of amusing stories to tell. Eventually, feeling that there was nothing to learn here, Darruwen took his leave and returned to his hut.

Only now, when he was sure that the Mage was out of earshot did Trethiwr's tone change.

"I have grave tidings from the mainland, Urien," he confided. "Rome has grown stronger recently; they control all of the great southern sea, and their influence extends east through the lands of the Helleni and south to the red lands on the far shore of the southern sea. We already know they control all of Iberia and now they threaten to push into Gaul. Only the lack of a great war leader holds them up. They are not like us; we fight amongst ourselves as willingly as against foreign tribes. They fight together as one for what they call their nation. While we fiercely maintain our freedom and independence they unite, and subjugate one tribe after another, bringing each one under their absolute control before moving on to the next tribe. They are like a swarm of ants carrying off larger insects one by one, to devour them in the nest, before re-emerging to repeat the process, again and again."

"Our Mage warned against you," said Urien. "There will come among us, one who has deserted us and now returns with false prophesies of war and destruction," Urien quoted the Mage.

"I am hardly a deserter!" protested Trethiwr. "I'm a traveller, a trader, an envoy, an explorer, but a sworn subject to you, Urien."

"Well, you choose a word, he chooses another word, but you do come with prophesies of war and destruction."

"But not false prophesies," countered Trethiwr.

"So you claim. But what danger are the Romani to me?"

"The Keltoi are not a nation, we are not all one tribe. We share a similar language and culture, we agree on laws, and customs, and Gods, although all of those can change from tribe to tribe. But at least with us, if one tribe defeats another there is only tribute to pay. We keep our lands, the land we farm ourselves. We keep our freedom, to plant and harvest when we choose, to be ourselves, to fight and drink and hunt and love. Kano-Walo would never come here and tell you how to run your village, just so long as you pay the tribute. The Romani don't just conquer and exact tribute: they completely overwhelm. They leave soldiers and governors who rule over the local king. They take over the land and make slaves of the people who work it. Their leaders declare ownership over lands they not only have never worked on, but have never even seen. All the grain and timber and livestock and valuable metals will be sent to Rome. The rich will get richer while the poor can starve. They play off one tribal leader against another, using us against ourselves until they have the strength to take over everything. You can't trust them, you can't bargain with them, you can't be their ally. Not for long anyway."

"What would you have me do?" enquired Urien.

"Build alliances, not with war but with words. Come with me to Maywr-Dun first and we will ask Kano-Walo to lead us."

Urien protested vociferously.

"That dog!" I'd rather be skinned alive!"

"Would you rather become a slave to the Romani?"

"I would die first!" stated Urien, truthfully.

"Yes and so would all your people, your wives, your children, everything you know and love, for what? Pride?"

"Are they so strong?" asked Urien, incredulously. "Did not Brynno defeat them in their own city?"

"Look," Trethiwr tried to conceal his exasperation, like a parent explaining a simple problem to a small child, "you can cut down an oak sapling with one swift stroke of the axe. But a full-grown tree will take all the axes of the clan working together. Brynno had an army of more than one clan. More than one tribe! There were warriors from the Boii, as well as his own Sennoni, and the mercenaries, and our own ancestor Pretano with his clan. Only if we can stand united, like our ancestors did, do we stand a chance."

"But," continued Urien, "you say they lack a great war-leader? Then they cannot be a threat." Urien felt this settled everything.

"I have studied the secret arts for many years," said Trethiwr. "When Blyth was born I sought prophecies for his fate. I found more than I bargained for. A lamb I sacrificed had what looked like two hearts. I read this to mean there is another boy born on the same day; their fates are entwined."

Urien spoke, "A very strange prophesy indeed."

"That night I had a dream," said Trethiwr. "A pack of wolves appeared in a clearing by a stream. As I watched them, a lone wolf appeared and tried to join the pack. They attacked him and he fled, but he kept close by on the edge of the forest.

The wolves were edgy and nervous. They kept looking across the stream, their fur was standing up and teeth bared. Occasionally they fought with each other, just little skirmishes, as if fighting over who should be pack leader.

Then another pack appeared, slowly, out of a clump of trees on the other side of the stream. They moved together as one, led by the alpha male, a sleek grey with bright amber eyes. They crossed the stream right into the territory of the first pack - most unnatural behaviour for wolves. There was a fierce fight; fur flew and blood spilled, wolves lay dead and dying on both sides. Eventually the first pack was forced to retreat, leaving the territory for the stronger invaders. Their victory was short lived, for out of the trees came the lone wolf. Yet even as he attacked, the dream faded and I woke up, the outcome yet to be revealed."

Trethiwr spread his hands and sat back.

"I confess I did not know what this meant then and I only have a slight idea now. But the wolves are the reason I named my first son Blyth. I now believe that the boy whose destiny is twinned with Blyth's is the alpha male, and that he has some connection with wolves, and Blyth is represented by the lone wolf."

"Well it's a great fireside story, Trethiwr," said Urien, unconvinced. "I will need time to think things over."

Urien stood and Trethiwr took the signal to depart, along with Epona, who had remained silent all this time, but had listened intently to every word.

5

Over the next few days the weather worsened; chill winds came in from the north blowing huge dark clouds, piled up in the sky, blotting out the sun for days and weeping freezing rain upon the desolate landscape. Then the wind direction changed to an easterly which brought heavy snow in its wake. The whiteness blanketed the ground to the horizon in every direction and the cold was constant, biting, merciless.

Travel was out of the question and the village huddled on the hilltop, buffeted by every gust of wind and dusted with every flurry of snow. Drifts piled up in the defensive ditches, filling them up, making all the ground appear level. Snowdrops, camouflaged - almost buried against the whiteness - did their best to offer their wares to any insane insects that might be airborne. Some of the blossom on the fruit trees was emerging, thanks to the unusually warm start of the year, but was now cut down by severe frost, thus reducing the crop for later in the year. Ploughing ceased and planting would have to wait. The calves arrived anyway; the herd was brought into the fort away from the worst of the blizzards. The same applied when the lambing season began and the village seemed extremely overcrowded; people jostling side by side with cows, sheep, pigs, goats, and the usual chickens, along with pet hares and geese. This standoff continued until the next full moon; the people of Ba-Dun held hostage by the whim of the Gods.

By the time the worst of the bad weather had receded and the snows began to thaw, there was an urgent need to replenish food supplies. The woods and fields around Ba-Dun were teeming with game, all in search of the same thing, and hunters went out in several parties armed with bows, slings, and spears, to capture anything that would move. Likewise they sought any root vegetables that might add some bulk to the pot and carried tools for digging as well.

Trethiwr led his sons into the woods for the first time in his life. They had been hunting before, with their uncle, and now Trethiwr was looking forward to seeing what they could do and also showing them a trick or two that he had up his sleeve. Within a few minutes of silent movement among the thin trees at the edge of the forest Trethiwr spotted a nesting wood dove. It had seen them coming some way off and was as still as a statue. Perfectly blended with the tree it inhabited, it was almost impossible to see. In fact Abbon still could not see it as Trethiwr encouraged Blyth to take aim with his small bow. Blyth took careful aim but the pressure of taking the first shot, of trying to impress his father and his brothers, was too much for him. The shot went wide and low, hitting the bough and bouncing off. The bird took flight into much higher branches. Abbon was all for climbing up to see if there were any eggs but Trethiwr wanted to keep moving in pursuit of something bigger.

Blyth appeared crushed by his failure.

"Forget it," his father said, breaking the hunting silence. "Show me a hunter who has never missed, and I'll show you a hunter who has never taken a shot! Come now. Silence, and we will find more game soon enough."

Trethiwr led the way towards where, he recalled from his many trips in these woods, there was a track used by grazing animals. It led to a stream where large animals like boar and deer would go to drink. Downwind as they were, and daubed with cow dung to mask their scent, they watched as a young roe deer approached, oblivious to the danger. The deer, a female, still in her winter coat, a dark greyish brown, sniffed the air suspiciously. She was lean, clearly having had a hard time of the last few weeks. You could almost count her ribs but then again there would still be more than a feast even on that thin frame. Teague was eager to take a shot and Abbon was weighing a couple of sharp stones but

Trethiwr stayed their hands and signalled to Blyth to take aim. Blyth was reluctant, having failed so miserably before, but he hefted a javelin for balance before hurling it hard at the deer. At almost that same moment however, the loud chattering of a magpie in the tree above them spooked the animal which leapt high in the air causing the point to miss by a whisker. In the next bound the beast was gone; the magpie lay at their feet, skewered neatly by one of Trethiwr's arrows.

"Cursed bird!" Trethiwr swore through gritted teeth.

Blyth was crushed. Twice he had failed out of two attempts. He was useless, not worthy to hunt, fit only for domestic work, grooming horses and cleaning out pigsties. He sat on the floor, his knees pulled up close to his chest and head bowed down with his hands on the back of his neck, rocking back and forth.

Trethiwr watched Blyth, and saw himself as a young man having failed to mount a horse, three times in a row, in front of the whole village. He remembered the feeling of utter humiliation, of just wanting the ground to open and swallow him up; everyone else could do it so easily and he had made it look like the hardest thing on earth. The young colt had skipped and flicked its tail imperiously as he picked himself up out of the dirt, bruised both physically and mentally. He had walked away to the hut and hid under his mother's spare cloak. It was Kaito who came and forced him to try again, Kaito who persuaded him that failure was not failure until you gave up trying, Kaito who breathed a charm into the colt before Trethiwr attempted to mount for the fourth time. This time the colt moved with him, and he with it, in a smooth, fluid motion. He was like a centaur; a man as one with a horse.

"Come on forget it," Trethiwr said.

"We should eat and drink, we will feel better afterwards and then, perhaps, I will show you a few tricks you won't have learned from your uncle."

They stopped in a gap between a circle of oaks, overgrown with grass and woodland flowers.

While they ate, Trethiwr tried to bolster Blyth's confidence. Then he told some funny stories which made the boys laugh, scaring any game for miles around. Then, when they had finished and packed things away, Trethiwr told them to wait there and he walked to the middle of the clearing and drew his sword - the first time he had done so since Urien gave it to him a month ago.

He held the sword up in front of him, point downwards, grasped just below the hilt, and whispered a few unintelligible words. Then he drew a circle in the air with the tip of the sword, speaking some more words of power and magic.

He sheathed the sword and moved silently back to where the boys sat watching him with ill-concealed bemusement. Trethiwr was obviously back in hunting mode. He offered no explanation but signalled they should move into the trees which they did silently, as hunters again.

He signalled that they should deal with the magpie. It was considered unfit to eat; Trethiwr had only shot it as a reflex action against its untimely interruption to the hunt. He offered a prayer to the Gods and buried the bird. It was wrong to hunt a creature which could not be eaten or used in some way. The ceremony was needed to ensure the hunt would not be ruined.

Then they sat and waited, watching the invisible circle drawn by Trethiwr in the clearing; Blyth, miserable and sceptical, Teague curious and sceptical, Abbon sceptical and bored. Less than half an hour passed and then, from out of the trees, a wild boar trotted as bold as brass, straight to the middle of the clearing. As it walked into the circle there was a shimmer in the air like the heat haze of a fire, and the boar stood completely still.

Trethiwr signalled for Teague and Abbon to wait and clearly indicated for Blyth to take the shot. Blyth signalled a negative and folded his arms, looking downcast. Trethiwr signalled to the others to sit still, which he did also. Teague and Abbon obeyed unwillingly. It was deeply ingrained, to obey signals from the leader of the hunt without question. Blyth's behaviour was against this conditioning, but then he was obviously very unhappy.

As they waited another boar and then a small roe deer walked calmly into the circle from different sides of the clearing. Both animals joined the first boar inside the ring of power and the air shimmered as they passed the boundary drawn by Trethiwr's sword. Blyth stared at the three creatures as they stood completely still together, his mouth and eyes wide open. They were unnaturally calm and seemed to ignore each other. It was the strangest sight he had ever seen. Trethiwr smiled at him and offered his bow to Blyth, ready knocked with the best arrow he had. Blyth hesitated and Trethiwr gave him a clear signal: take the shot NOW!

Blyth pulled back on the string and loosed the arrow straight into the neck of the first boar. It leaped and writhed yet did not leave the circle. More astonishingly the other two animals stood motionless, as if hypnotized or drugged, never once reacting to the dying boar beside them.

The first animal lay still and Trethiwr signalled to Abbon to have a go. Abbon used his favourite weapon, a sling, and took aim at the deer. The first stone missed by inches, the second struck above the deer's left ear. Abbon was not put off by this and the animal appeared not to have noticed. His third shot hit right between the eyes, and the deer, concussed, slowly collapsed and lay motionless. This left Teague; he was the most curious and was more interested to know more about the spell that bound the last remaining boar than in actually killing the beast. He stepped cautiously out of the cover of trees and into the clearing. The boar looked straight at him yet did not flee. He walked right up to the edge of the circle and stood there. He could reach out and touch the boar's flank. He could run his hand along its back and feel its coarse bristles; the boar accepted this with the same lack of reaction as it had shown to everything else. The haze around the circle flickered a little and Trethiwr signalled to Teague to hurry up. Finally, he decided to dispatch the beast and ask questions later. He held his spear aloft and drove it forcefully into the neck of the passive boar. It was all over in a minute or two.

The four huntsmen returned to Ba-Dun with extreme difficulty, laden as they were with such an unnaturally successful haul. Other parties had met with mixed success but the return of Trethiwr and his sons with no less than two boar and a deer caused a tremendous stir.

Most people were pleased, a few were jealous, one or two were suspicious. Darruwen was furious but did not let his feelings be known. The village ate well that night and Trethiwr was treated as Urien's guest of honour, seated on one side of him with Darruwen on the other.

The next day Trethiwr spoke to Epona about his plans.

"I have only just returned and we have had so little time together, yet now I must ask you to leave here. Only through unity can our people stop the prophesied Roman invasion. Our people prize freedom but with that freedom comes division. The Romani subjugate themselves to the authority of the state, but because of that they can raise a huge army and support that army through victory or defeat. As long as our tribes fight against each other the Romani will use that weakness to defeat first one and then another tribe until they have all the land in their power. They will make slaves of our brave warriors, and exact tributes and taxes that will leave our people weak and hungry. It will be an end of freedom in this land, perhaps forever."

Trethiwr paused, but Epona offered no comment so he continued.

"I need you to go to your brother, in the east, to the Eceni Mawr. You can persuade him that the danger is real and he may be able to convince the King there."

Epona nodded.

"You should take Elarch with you," added Trethiwr. "She will be... happier with you." He had been going to say safer, but changed the word at the last moment. Epona noticed the hesitation but seemingly ignored it.

"I will leave in the morning," she said. "Now let us enjoy each other's company for one night shall we?" she added, as she passed him a mead cup and they drank to Toutatis, beseeching him to preserve the tribe.

In the morning Epona packed everything she would need for a long journey. She bade farewell to Blyth, Teague, and Abbon. They were sad and begged her not to go. Trethiwr was still almost a stranger to them and their mother was the only person in the tribe who cared more about them than anything else. Blyth was stony faced and angry, Teague was puzzled and tearful,

Abbon insisted on going with them, then insisted they stayed. Despite their protests, Epona fixed her bags to a dark brown pack horse, and Elarch rode a small pure white pony. She had a natural affinity for horses and rode better than many a young warrior. Epona, it seemed, was planning to walk, as there were only the two animals. "Perhaps," thought Blyth, "she is not going far."

They watched Epona lead the pack horse and Elarch's pony through the village gates and down the track, past the ridges and ditches which formed the defences, and off down the hillside. Blyth continued to watch, even after they were out of sight in the woodlands. He knew that in an hour or so they would emerge from the trees at the crest of the next hill, following the high path that lead all the way to the far eastern edge of Pretan. Then they would disappear over the hill and he would not see them again... for how long, he did not know. As Blyth watched the far distant hilltop he finally made out three figures moving swiftly at a canter. A dark coloured pack horse, a snow white pony with a small rider, and what looked like a pale horse, with a long reddish gold mane, leading the group. Blyth closed his eyes tight and re-opened them, and the three horses disappeared over the horizon. He must have imagined it, he thought.

6

Preparations were made for a delegation to Maywr-Dun over the next few days. A messenger was sent to inform Kano-Walo of Urien's intentions. The watch at Maywr-Dun would see their party approaching from miles away, and a large party might be perceived as a raid and warriors sent out to attack.

As soon as the messenger returned, the next day, with Kano-Walo's approval for the meeting, Urien set off with his entourage. Trethiwr was there of course, and the Mage insisted on coming. Kyndyrn was there as Urien's champion, and several other warriors including Rodokoun. They rode horses, and looked very fine in brightly coloured woollen cloaks, tunics, and trousers. Shields were slung over their backs, horn shaped, in the fashion of the village, and brightly coloured with their insignia. Torcs and spear points glinted in the sunlight. All together there were fifty men and women in the group which rode with Urien to negotiate at Maywr-Dun.

Kano-Walo was at the main gate to the fortress with his champion, Lugovalos, and three Mages - Kanvodur, the seer, Gurandur, the listener, and Siaradur, the speaker - as well as a host of warriors on horseback.

Kano-Walo greeted Urien in a formal way, nodded recognition to Trethiwr and accompanied the party into Maywr-Dun. His warriors mingled with those of Urien; two horsemen to each one of Urien's. Maywr-Dun was a magnificent fortress; twice the size of Ba-Dun inside the fence. The surrounding earthworks consisted of at least four or five ridges and ditches, each ridge built up to more than three times the height of a man, and the ditches similarly deep. There were stone walls at the top of the central ridges which could be defended and, if necessary, abandoned for the larger inner walls. These were of huge dry stones built up around a timber palisade of oak stakes, as thick as a man's thigh, sharpened to points at the top. Behind this there were piles of smaller stones for use with slings and larger stones which could be cast onto the closest attackers.

There were scores of buildings: family roundhouses, grain stores raised on stilts, workshops, storehouses, and communal buildings. The population of Maywr-Dun was around fifty-times-fifty people including warriors, landowners, skilled workers and their servants. Outside the walls, in the surrounding fields, there were many more people who worked the land and paid tribute to the Chief. These were mainly the descendants of people who had lived on this land for generations before the Keltoi had arrived from the continent and taken over. There was a network of paths leading in different directions, but the group now made their way along the main road to the great central clearing where the Chief's hut stood. This was larger than any building in Ba-Dun and had stone walls coated in a thick layer of hard dried mud and dung. This was painted white, with lime, and on this background was a pattern of red and black wavy lines.

The top of the roof was fully four times the height of the biggest warrior in the tribe and the walls were almost twice his height. Inside there was a pair of bronze dogs which stood on either side of the fireplace and held an iron rod between their teeth. On this was supported a huge iron pot of water. There were furs piled on furs in the sleeping areas, which were separated from the main part of the hut by wicker walls with leather hinged doors. The inner walls were hung with huge woollen drapes which served as decoration as well as insulation.

But if the Chief's hut was impressive, it was as nothing compared to the temple. In Ba-Dun the temple was merely a circle of oak trees, the roof made of the overhung branches, the altar was a huge block of beech, carved with ancient symbols and scripts. The temple of Maywr-Dun stood at the eastern end of the central clearing. It appeared to be built of two huge roundhouses merged into one long rectangular building. The walls and roof were of similar proportions to those of the Chief's hut, being decorated with many sacred images and texts. Inside, the walls were covered with hangings depicting images of animals and various deities, created by sewing different coloured fabric shapes onto a base material of wool. In the centre was a stone altar, and a fire which was kept burning at all times.

Negotiations began in earnest and discussions centred first on whether the threat was from Roma, or perhaps closer to home. Chief Kano-Walo was suspicious and almost openly suggested that perhaps the real threat lay in Ba-Dun. He seemed warm and friendly to Trethiwr which aroused suspicion amongst Urien and those closest to him.

Trethiwr spoke eloquently about the Romani and how they were organised and united. He compared this to the free-spirited Pretani, who lacked any cohesion. He argued that even the most fearsome warrior was no match for a disciplined army, and that was what they would face when the Romani did invade. Meanwhile there was the increasing influx of Gallic tribes coming from the continent and settling in areas mainly to the east, where they had already taken over from the original tribes there. There was a moment of agreement between the two great Chiefs when they almost decided to organise an army to attack the Belgae as they were called but this unravelled when Urien insisted on being joint leader, while Kano-Walo could not allow for more than a supporting role for the lesser Chief.

All the while the three Mages sat just behind the Chief: Kanvodur in the centre of the three, his eyes glazed over, his mind seemingly in another place, Gurandur on his left, carefully taking in the conversation, and Siaradur, gaining insight from the other two and whispering advice to Kano-Walo from time to time.

After days of arguing back and forth it appeared that nothing had been achieved except a confirmation of what everybody already knew; that the peace between Ba-Dun and Maywr-Dun was merely a product of bountiful harvests, which made farming more rewarding than warfare… as long as it lasted. Eventually Urien decided to leave and give up on Trethiwr's crazy plans. Darruwen had finally got his way, which was to maintain the present state of affairs. He saw the threat from the continent as minor, but the threat to himself from Trethiwr as being more serious. He knew Trethiwr possessed magical skills far superior to his own and feared he might want to take over as Mage. He needed to ensure that Trethiwr failed to unite the tribes and more importantly he needed to get rid of Trethiwr by any means possible. In the temple he spoke with Gurandur, the Listener.

"I have sought prophesies and it saddens me that I have to conclude there will be trouble between our clans. I want no part of this trouble and I believe that deep down Urien also seeks peace with Kano-Walo and his kin."

The Listener lived up to his name and did not interrupt.

Darruwen continued, "I feel certain that the cause of all this trouble is Trethiwr, who is recently come among us after many years away. Our long period of good harvests and prosperity can be measured from the time of his departure and just recently we have had bitter cold, and wind, and snow, and ice, just after he came back."

Kanvodur, the seer, had arrived and Gurandur looked to him for confirmation of this prophesy.

"I have seen fighting between our clans and it saddens me also. Many are the kinships between us so that a war will be as brother fighting with brother. I have not seen the root of the trouble, but as you have said Trethiwr has recently returned and with him comes the worst spring in my memory. It may well be a sign."

"What would you suggest, Darruwen?" Gurandur asked.

"Kano-Walo should take hostages to ensure Urien's faithful service. It is unfortunate, but there is no other way. Leave Trethiwr though, and give Urien leave to return with him and the rest of the party. Trethiwr will be blamed for the hostages and it will be simple to persuade Urien that he is also the reason for the bad weather and perhaps I can convince the clan that he is plotting with Kano-Walo. They already think that he is too friendly with your Chief."

Gurandur nodded but did not speak.

Darruwen went on, "After a few months, once Trethiwr is dealt with, we can work to foster better relations between our clans. By Belotenios we will be firm allies once more."

Siaradur, the speaker, arrived at this point and he swiftly took in the details of the conversation from the other two.

"I will speak to Kano-Walo," he declared and he went to advise his Chief.

Urien's party were preparing to leave, packing bags and seeing to the horses, when Kano-Walo came to them with a large force of warriors.

"I require you to leave me ten hostages, to ensure your faithfulness to me and my clan," he declared, recycling the words spoken to him moments before by Siaradur.

Kano-Walo's forces moved swiftly among the unprepared visitors.

"What nonsense is this?" called Urien above the rising hubbub.

Already ten of his warriors, including Rodokoun and his elder sister Rhuthgem, were cut off from the rest, like sheep separated by a pack of dogs.

The move was slick and well planned; fifty armed warriors surrounded the ten. Another fifty stood facing Urien and his remaining party, spears held ready to strike.

Urien knew he had been outmanoeuvred and his resistance could not gain anything but death for him and complete subjugation for his clan. He swore an oath inside his head to avenge this treachery and outwardly he fixed a fierce smile on his face and spoke to Kano-Walo who was there with sword drawn.

"My cousin!" he implored. They both claimed descent from the grandson of Pretan who was killed with Brynno, which made them seventh cousins. "How can you make such an accusation? I seek nothing but unity and peace between our clans. We have many family ties; why would I seek a war with you?"

"I have my advice," declared Kano-Walo, never once taking his eyes off Urien.

While this exchange was going on, Rodokoun was becoming increasingly angry. He was young, and had never used his sword or spear in battle. He was itching to slash the stupid grins off the faces of the two older warriors who stood before him, with spears held at the ready. His sword was, however, in its sheath strapped to his horse, which stood some distance away awaiting his departure, along with his spears and shield. If he could just move quickly enough and reach his sword...

Meanwhile, one of the warriors facing his sister, Rhuthgem, was paying her more attention than was required simply for guarding her. He reached out and pulled her towards him by the lapels of her travelling cloak. "Welcome to Maywr-Dun," he said in a rough voice and he tried to kiss her. She recoiled and fell backwards onto the muddy ground. A few of the guards laughed and while their attention was drawn Rodokoun dived between his guards for his horse.

He leapt into the saddle and slid his sword from the sheath in one fluid motion that he had practised countless times. He turned his horse and hacked clean through the head of his sister's tormentor. His next sweep parried two spears in one movement and his third cut across the chests of his own two guards. It was his last conscious movement; three spears thrust from different points around him skewered his torso. His lifeless body sat balanced by the weight of the spears on his horse.

The rest of Urien's party had been swiftly subdued and their arms taken beyond all possible reach. Kyndyrn had to be held by four men as he struggled to help his young kinsman. The remaining hostages were taken away, Rhuthgem screaming all the while for her baby brother. Trethiwr stood motionless throughout, his magic powerless to stop the bloodshed once it had started. Only Urien was still fighting. He had taken a sword from the nearest guard and stood now with his back to a large hut, holding off all comers with a strength and skill born of fury.

Trethiwr watched him intently, casting protective spells over his Chief. A ring of warriors surrounded him as he stood with his back to the hut wall but none could come close enough to subdue him. A number of spears were thrown but each was parried by the old Chief as if it flew in slow motion. It appeared that the standoff would last for some time and then suddenly a sword was thrust through from the inside of the hut, running Urien through from back to front. His face registered complete surprise, then the sword was pulled swiftly out and he collapsed in front of the wall.

Darruwen rushed forwards; this was the last thing he had expected or intended. He bent over the still form of his Chief and tried to see how bad the wound was, he hoped vaguely that it was perhaps not as bad as it looked. There was a lot of blood but the Chief still lived. The Mage tore open the tunic and was startled to see there was no sign of any wound. It was in fact the power of Trethiwr's amulet, the little golden cross with the loop at the top, which had healed Urien's wound but Darruwen never wasted an opportunity to make himself look good. He quickly placed his hand over the place where the deep gash should have been and muttered a healing charm. Covering up the supposed wound he turned the Chief towards the silent waiting crowd and checked his back. Similarly there was a lot of blood but he could find no sign of an entry wound. He spoke more healing charms, louder this time, and a smile crossed his face. Urien's eyes flickered open and Darruwen helped him to his feet. He had no idea how it had happened but the man who, in front of dozens of witnesses, had been run clean through with a sword stood before them without a mark on his body. As far as everyone could tell, Darruwen had healed fatal wounds before their very eyes.

He turned and took control of the situation.

"We will leave now and let no man or woman try to stop us."

He turned to Kano-Walo.

"Your men have dealt us a great wrong by killing our youngest warrior. You have taken nine hostages from us and now you must give us the three who dealt the fatal blows to Rodokoun, in return."

Darruwen looked fiercely around at the assembled warriors and then back at Kano-Walo.

"You have seen the powers of healing that I possess. Now give us what I ask or you will see the powers of destruction that I may unleash!"

This was of course a hollow threat but nobody knew that except, perhaps, Trethiwr, who remained silent.

Kano-Walo indicated that the three warriors, two men and a woman, who had thrown the spears should do as Darruwen demanded.

Rodokoun was carefully lifted down from his horse and the spears pulled from his body. He was placed on a bier and the three were made to carry it from Maywr-Dun before loading it onto a wagon for the journey back to Ba-Dun

7

The return journey was a sorrowful one. Nothing had been achieved except the death of a young hero and the loss of nine clan members. Tension between the two powerful clans was greater than ever and perhaps only the hostages kept them from an outright war.

A mile or so from Ba-Dun Urien urged his horse into a gallop followed by Kyndyrn. Darruwen did not follow; he wanted to keep an eye on Trethiwr. Trethiwr rode slowly near the back, speaking to no-one, lost in his thoughts.

When the main party arrived back at the village, Urien had already warned the people what to expect. There was great mourning, especially by Cuilleana, Rodokoun's mother, who had lost her only son, gone to feast with Lugh, and her only daughter, hostage to Maywr-Dun.

Preparations were made for a funeral fit for a

warrior and hero. Darruwen prepared the body, and the ritual took place on the evening of the day after Rodokoun's death. They built a fire around a platform, on which Rodokoun's body was placed. This was done to the west of the village on a slight raised area of land. Pots were placed with him containing oil, honey, and mead; bread and meat were provided also. His sword and shield were laid beside him and three good throwing spears, a knife and his best torc of twisted copper and silver wire. All these would be needed in the young warrior's next life.

The fire was lit, having been very carefully laid to ensure the flames would take hold quickly. It soon engulfed the stylised boat, which would follow Bellenos, the Sun God, across the western sea and over the edge of this world, into the next. The villagers watched the fire for some time, while Trethiwr took Blyth aside and spoke to him very seriously.

"I need you to promise me something Blyth." He spoke quietly but firmly, "I know I have never been much of a father to you, but I am going to ask more of you than any father has a right to ask of his son, not just for me but for the clan and for the tribe and for all the Pretani."

Blyth looked concerned.

"What do you want me to do?" he asked.

"I will be blamed for Rodokoun's death," said Trethiwr, simply. "No don't interrupt," he added, seeing Blyth was about to protest. "I will be blamed for that, and for the recent spell of cold weather, and for the hostages as well. Darruwen will see to it. Everybody witnessed Darruwen appear to heal Urien's fatal wounds. Nobody will believe the truth that it was the Ankh that I gave to him, the amulet, the symbol of life. I have sworn an oath of allegiance to Urien and I must obey the law. My place in the next world depends on what I do in this." Trethiwr looked thoughtful for a moment, "You have to take Teague and Abbon with you and leave Ba-Dun forever. Your future lies elsewhere. You may never see me again."

"Where will we go? What future? What use will I be to the clan, to the tribe, to the Pretani? Why can't I... ?" Questions tumbled out of Blyth's mouth one after the other, but Trethiwr held up his hand for silence.

"You have an important task to fulfil. You will know what to do in the proper time. First you must go back to my grandfather, Kaito. Go back to the woods where you met him the first time. He can only be found when he wants to be found. He will be waiting for you there. You must do what he tells you. You will learn many forms of magic and you will train with the Deru-Weidi, the order of the wise oak Mages."

"Are they like Darruwen? He is named after the oak." Said Blyth.

"No," replied Trethiwr, "They are much more powerful than our Mage; as indeed you will be. Your destiny brings you into conflict with a man with some connection to wolves, I still do not know what this means and more than this I cannot tell you."

Trethiwr paused again.

"Promise me though that, whatever happens, you will make sure that you and Teague and Abbon go straight away, to find Kaito."

Blyth hesitated.

"PROMISE!" Trethiwr hissed.

"I promise." Said Blyth.

"Or may the sky fall down on you," added Trethiwr. "Say it!" he commanded

"Or may the sky fall down on me," muttered Blyth reluctantly.

"That is enough I think," said Trethiwr, "Come on, let us head back."

The villagers were returning to the fortress. The flames would burn for many hours to come and in the morning they would return to dispose of the remains. Blyth spoke to Teague and Abbon on the way back to the village and repeated what Trethiwr had told him. Teague had a lot of questions; Abbon had a few flippant comments. Blyth shut them both up when he told them he had sworn by the sky to leave the village.

"You can't just leave us," insisted Teague.

"You're coming with me, both of you," said Blyth.

There was a stunned silence followed by an outburst of protest from both younger brothers.

"Look, Father made me swear to take both of you away from here as soon as possible. I suggest you pack quickly, and travel light."

As soon as they arrived back they began to sort out the things they would need to take. Abbon packed his sling and a small knife given to him by one of the older warriors. Teague packed a set of pieces and a board for a game that Trethiwr had learned on his travels. He and Blyth had carved it with Trethiwr during their father's last visit. Trethiwr had seen the game played, and taught Blyth the rules. But it was Teague who was the better player, despite being only five when he first learned. He seldom played now as Blyth had lost interest after being repeatedly beaten. Only Epona among the clan was able to play and she was often busy. But the set reminded him of his father and mother; both of whom would be gone for a long time. Blyth sought out his torc of twisted silver and copper wires. He made sure they had plenty of tinder and a kit for making fire, his bow and some arrows, sinew, a knife and some coins left by Epona. Since he had no idea what he might need, he decided the currency would be more flexible. Besides if he was never coming back then nor would his mother, he presumed. He took whatever jewellery he could find as well, a few brooches and some arm torcs.

Evening was drawing in, and it was too late to leave on a journey. The boys settled down on Epona's furs and wondered where their father was on this, their last night together for some time. They ate some strips of smoked boar; there was at least plenty of food since their successful hunt.

The village was bustling with people. Some watched

the funeral pyre burning in the west, mingled with the last of the sunset, a few were drinking mead outside their houses, but quite a few were gathered in the central clearing. Darruwen was speaking to a large group of elders and seasoned warriors.

"Trethiwr has brought nothing but bad luck to this village," he argued, to general nods and murmurs of agreement. "But there is worse. Trethiwr plots against Urien with none other than Kano-Walo. This whole disaster at Maywr-Dun was engineered by Trethiwr as a way of getting us to become vassals to them. He thinks that by delivering us bound and gagged, Kano-Walo will become High Chief - King over all the Dwr-Y-Tryges - and he, Trethiwr the traitor, will become high Mage over all other Mages."

There was much outrage at this, and menacing threats from angry warriors. Nobody could doubt the word of the Mage who had, only three days ago, saved the life of Chief Urien from a fatal wound.

"He must be punished," continued Darruwen, "and a sacrifice must be made to appease the Gods. Until this is done there is no possibility of peace or prosperity in our land."

The warriors stood around unsure what to do next, looking to Darruwen for instructions.

"Bring him to the temple," ordered the Mage. "I will wait for you there."

The warriors departed and searched for Trethiwr.

Darruwen went to the temple to prepare. Here he

found Trethiwr waiting for him.

"I thought you would never come," he said as Darruwen appeared in the circle of trees. He stood relaxed and calm in front of the altar. A plain undyed tunic and sandals were all he wore. Darruwen looked haunted. He gripped his amber-topped staff tightly and glanced around him for the warriors but they were gone, searching for the man who stood before him now.

"I know what is to be," Trethiwr said without a trace of emotion.

"Go on," replied the Mage.

"You see me as a threat. You seek to rid yourself of me, once and for all. Sadly, for you and for the clan, you are wrong. Wrong about the source of threat and wrong about the cause of your bad luck."

The Mage interrupted. "Wrong or not, the sadness is for you not for me."

"Again you are mistaken, Darruwen, for soon I will feast with Lugh. Your journey to the other world will begin sooner than you think but you will wander long before you join me."

Darruwen sneered. "I doubt very much that Lugh will greet you at his table without arms, without food or wine, without torcs or clothes!"

"My wealth is in my head," said Trethiwr. "I have walked with Lugh before, in a far-off land, but there is no time to tell the story now. Look; your dogs are back."

Sure enough, several warriors were here to inform Darruwen that they could not find Trethiwr. A few had already left to advise the rest to call off the search. Urien came to the temple, brought by another messenger, and Darruwen ordered Trethiwr to be bound and gagged, speaking to Urien while this was done.

"This man has been plotting with Kano-Walo to make him high King of all the Dwr-Y-Tryges," he declared. "He has brought the death of Rodokoun, and the loss of nine warriors, held hostage at Maywr-Dun. He brought with him the worst cold and snow in living memory, and he almost caused your own death. He must be punished and a sacrifice must be made to appease the Gods," declared Darruwen. "I believe that Trethiwr himself should be the sacrifice."

A few gasps went up: there had not been a human sacrifice for some time and never before a close relative of the Chief.

"I have no opinion on the business of the Gods," announced Urien.

This was his only option. The Mage held the ultimate power in the clan. If he openly expressed a strong opinion then the Chief was obliged to agree to it. A Chief who publicly opposed the Mage would not be Chief for long. Besides, if Trethiwr was plotting against him, then Urien would be better off with him out of the way. Trethiwr gave no reaction; it was as if he knew this was coming. He only hoped that Blyth had already left with Teague and Abbon, and would not witness this.

Darruwen took out a drinking skin from his cloak and forced Trethiwr to drink its contents. He ordered

65

the warriors to drag the condemned man from the temple. Following behind the Mage they dragged him through the village; many others joined the procession, bringing torches with them as it was dark now. The story of what was going on was passed from one villager to another. As the procession passed out of the gates Blyth, who had drifted into sleep, woke up and realised something was happening. He quickly got up and followed at a distance. At the gates he climbed the unmanned defences to see what was going on. He could just make out a figure, bound and gagged, being dragged to the edge of the woods to the north, where the river ran through the trees. The ground there was very wet and boggy. As the figure turned, Blyth recognised his father's face bathed in pale moonlight and he gasped in shock. He ran down the steps to the gates and dashed out to try and stop what was going to happen. At that point he ran straight into Cuilleana. She was tall and muscular and Blyth fell backwards to the floor. Of all the people to bump into she was the worst. How could he tell her that he wanted to save his father when she had just lost both her children and believed that his father was to blame?

He stood up and tried to move past her but she stepped in his path and held up her hand. When she spoke it was not with anger, but with tenderness.

"I know how you feel Blyth, but you cannot save him now. Darruwen has all the village on his side. You should be thinking of yourself and your brothers now.

Darruwen will realise that you must bear a grudge. He will try to find a way to get rid of all of you to avoid you seeking revenge in the future." She went on, "I loved Trethiwr once, when we were young, but your mother returned from far away and they matched perfectly, and who could compete with Epona for beauty? You have her face but your father's character. He was a great man and you will be even greater, but not if you go charging down that hill waving a spear you have never practised with. Impetuous; just like your father. He hated fighting but he had a wild temper in his youth. Later he travelled to the edge of the known world with no more protection than amulets and the power of his mind."

She held his hands in hers and spoke softly.

"For the sake of my son, for Rodokoun, leave now before they come back. Leave by the East gate, and get as far away as possible. Do you have horses?"

"One," said Blyth.

"Rodokoun will not be needing his two any more, but you will. Please take them, in memory of your father. You can pay me for them in the next world."

Blyth was immobile with indecision.

Cuilleana urged him on, "Go quickly, it will all be over soon and the villagers will be returning."

Blyth did as he was told and woke Teague and Abbon. They gathered their things and mounted the three horses. As a last thought, Blyth grabbed his father's sword.

"Where will you go?" asked Cuilleana.

"Father told us to seek a house in the woods. There is a Mage who lives alone there. I was told he would help us."

"Well I wish you luck," said Cuilleana, slapping his horse on the rump to get it going quickly.

"Thank you Cuilleana," called Blyth. "May Rodokoun travel swiftly to the house of Lugh, and may Rhuthgem marry a high King and bear many children!" he added.

While all this was happening, Trethiwr, drugged with potion and hallucinating, was stripped naked and held face down as four warriors with heavy clubs smashed his arms and legs, breaking the bones.

Darruwen twisted a strong sinew around Trethiwr's neck and pulled it tight, cutting deeply into the skin. As a thin red line appeared where the cord cut in, Trethiwr gurgled a little, the only noise he had uttered since his conversation with Darruwen in the temple. It was the sound of his soul leaving his body. Another blow of a club smashed his skull, and he was left face down in the filthy stinking mud. Finally another warrior thrust a spear through his back and at least a foot into the soil below. The spear was pulled out, and no goods were left with the body. The corpse might sink down into the mud or be eaten by animals, it did not matter. He would have nothing to take with him into the other world, if he ever made it there at all.

8

The three boys rode hard to the south, to avoid being seen by the villagers returning from the sacrifice. They headed quickly for the edge of the forest and rode quietly, skirting the edge of the trees towards the place where they had searched for firewood over a month before.

The night was warmer than recently; heavy clouds filled the sky making it a very dark night. Blyth had good night vision; Teague's was even better. He led the way; Abbon followed him, and Blyth brought up the rear. They didn't dare burn a torch. The air crackled with tension; as the horses stumbled through the undergrowth the first rain started to fall, in big fat heavy drops. It had that warm heady scent of pine and wood smoke, as it splashed on the young leaves and soaked into the boys' cloaks, and the horses' manes. Within minutes it was falling harder than Blyth had ever seen, crashing through the forest canopy like a sword through butter. The boys were drenched and cold. The horses continued, stoically, shivering and slipping on the wet ground. Lightning followed in great scything sheets, floodlighting the sky. Taranis, God of lightning, was busy and he had chosen a bad time for the boys.

With each flash of lightning, they could see the villagers silhouetted as they hurried back to the safety of the fortress. Blyth remembered his oath which he realized he had broken. "May the sky fall on my head," he had sworn when he promised his father that he would leave straight away. He had assumed that meant first thing in the morning, but now he suspected that his father had known all along what was going to happen. He had already sent Epona and Elarch away, and he had insisted that, "whatever happens," Blyth should take his brothers and leave.

Well the sky did seem to be collapsing on his head right now; it was as if someone was pouring buckets of water over them. Their clothes were soaked through to their skin and sagging with water. The horses looked miserable, barely able to see, and stumbling and splashing in muddy puddles. Another flash of lightning revealed Darruwen standing alone in the middle of an open field his right arm raised, holding his amber headed staff as high as he could, invoking Taranis, calling on him to cease his assault on the freshly ploughed and planted fields, and the huddled thatched huts.

The boys could not hear anything he was saying, even though he was shouting against the thunder and the hammering rain. Even as they watched, another bolt of lightning flashed and lit up the sky with Darruwen at the centre. His figure froze and then crumpled in a heap. Blyth gasped and searched the landscape to see if anyone had noticed but the rest of the villagers were all long gone and out of sight. He could not do anything. If the boys went back now they might well be blamed for the Mage's death. Someone would probably find the body in the morning when they went to inspect the damage to the fields.

The boys rode on with difficulty, cold, wet, and miserable, now pushing deeper into the forest. They argued about the right way to go. Blyth insisted he remembered a particular beech tree with an unusual branch; Teague recalled a rotted old oak. Abbon had been up in the trees the last time they had come this way, so nothing looked familiar to him. Eventually, when they thought they would surely drown in the ever growing puddles and streams that were springing up all over the forest floor, they spotted a feature they all recognized. The great ancient 'warrior oak' with the nine branched crown they had seen just before they first met Kaito. His house must be nearby. In the darkness they followed the scent of wood smoke and then the deep glow of the fire, still smoking and hissing away. It was brighter now than the last time they had seen it, glowing orange as they drew nearer through the trees. The horses were spooked, and kept stamping and whinnying frantically, rearing and backing away, for all the boys' efforts to control them. Abbon was thrown from the young pony that he was riding. Blyth and Teague just managed to stay on the more mature, better trained, mounts that Rodokoun's mother had lent them.

At that moment Kaito appeared and came quickly over. He whispered to the horses and they calmed instantly. He helped Abbon to his feet and retrieved the third horse by whistling a series of notes and whispering in its ear to calm it down. He led the three horses a short way to a partially covered enclosure, and the boys into his hut. They quickly took off their soaked clothes and Kaito gave them furs to keep them warm. The hut was unlike any they had ever seen. Outside it looked like a normal round house, with wattle and daub walls, whitewashed and decorated with familiar patterns. Inside there was no trace of smoke and it was warm and bone dry despite the cold and torrential rain outside. In the centre a fire crackled brightly with a hint of greenish blue. A large bronze pot, suspended from the middle of the roof, bubbled with a delicious smelling stew, and beeswax candles burned in bronze holders. Towards the back of the hut against the wall there was a row of shelves, with row upon row of small pots and even a number of glass bottles containing a bewildering array of different substances: different coloured liquids, dried plants, animal skins, fungi, insects, berries, powders, and stones. A hare sat on thick furs, on one of the ornately carved benches. It was well-fed and soft, and welcomed the boys' attention without flinching as they stroked it behind the ears.

Kaito bade them sit down and he gave them some of the stew in wooden bowls, with chunks of heavy, seedy bread. Then he went back outside to see to the horses. The shelter was constructed of several poles lashed together to form a large wide 'A' frame, enclosed on three sides with wattle and daub walls and a pole to tie the horses to. Kaito himself owned a large stallion, which was black with fierce eyes, and a two year old mare which was a grey, with large blue eyes, that looked melancholy. Next to these, the three horses that the boys had ridden looked very much the worse for the drenching they had received. They steamed gently in the shelter of the lean-to, looking thoroughly miserable. Kaito gave each horse a careful rub down. He had a special affinity with horses, and treated them with respect and love. The three perked up quite a bit after their grooming, and tucked into the food provided for them at the back of the shelter.

Back in the hut, Abbon and Teague were already asleep, curled up in their furs, and Blyth sat huddled by the fire with the hare in his lap, gently stroking its ears. Kaito took off his cloak in the doorway and shook the rain from it, hanging it up a little way from the fire. He put a pot of water over the fire then he went over and sat down next to Blyth.

"You should sleep," he said.

73

"I'm not sleepy," replied Blyth, truthfully.

The moon was nearly setting now. The rain was easing off and the storm had passed over, leaving the night outside as dark and quiet as a grave. The sun would rise in a few hours but Blyth would not sleep until he had unburdened himself of all his recent worries.

"My father, Trethiwr… your grandson," he added, pointedly.

Kaito listened patiently.

"He was dragged off by the Mage Darruwen, and the rest of the village. He was tied up and dragged along the ground. They were going to kill him. I couldn't do anything! I couldn't help him!" Blyth broke down in tears.

Kaito put an arm round his great grandson's shoulder but he shrugged it off.

Kaito stood and went over to the pot, which was steaming gently now. He added some powder from one of the bottles and some leaves from a stone jar and a heady scent rose from the pot. He stirred it slowly with a long silver rod and then, after a while, dipped two small drinking horns into the brew. Returning to Blyth he passed him one of the cups and took a sip from the other.

"Trethiwr predicted events, more accurately than even I thought," said Kaito. "We spoke frequently at length on many subjects."

"How?" asked Blyth incredulously. "He was away for six years and since he was back, there has not been a chance for him to visit you," he added.

"One of many things you will learn over the coming years," said Kaito.

"Years?" Blyth asked.

"Years!" the old man confirmed.

"But what about Father's plans to unite the tribes and fight the Romani?"

"Enough questions, Blyth. You need to sleep."

Blyth was feeling tired now; he had finished the sweet scented tea that Kaito gave him and his head was heavy and buzzing. Almost without warning he slumped on the furs, where he slept soundly. Kaito covered him with another fur and retired to a closed sleeping room on one side of the hut. Before sleeping he took out a wax tablet and on it he scratched a series of lines, the secret writing of the Deru-Weidi. Far away the corresponding wax tablet, now kept by Epona, duplicated the message. "Trethiwr is dead. Your boys are safe. Kaito."

In the morning it was Teague who woke first, as usual. He got up and took a look around. It took a little while for memories of the last night to come back to him, of the flight from the village, of the terrible storm, of seeing Darruwen struck by lightning. Then he remembered that his father was dead and that was why they were running away from home. His mother was away on a long journey and this was the hut of their great-grandfather, who should surely be dead of old age. Teague remembered the oldest woman he had ever known was Blodwyth's grandmother. It was said that she was over fifty. She had wrinkled skin and her hair was white as snow, her back was bent and when she walked it was slowly and with considerable pain. Teague worked out that Kaito must be at least eighty years old and yet he moved with ease and grace and although he was white haired and wrinkled, his eyes sparkled and he stood straight and tall.

Kaito stirred in his sleeping quarters and, after a cough and a stretch, came out to the main part of the hut.

"Good morning Teague," he said genially, as he bustled about putting various herbs together for an infusion. He filled a pot and put it over the fire which had seemingly not died down in the night. It crackled merrily with the same smokeless flame, orange with a blue-green tinge to it. When Kaito had filled two horns with the brew, he passed one to Teague and sat with the other himself. Teague eyed the drink suspiciously.

"What's in this?" he asked.

"Drink, it's good; it will wake you up."

"I'm awake," Teague pointed out rather obviously. "What's in it?"

"A blend of herbs to invigorate and refresh. Drink."

Teague sat and eyed the hot liquid as if it might be some kind of poison.

Kaito sipped his own drink delicately, and breathed deeply, enjoying the aroma. Teague sniffed it and thought he could make out mint, and a sharp smell he did not recognize. Kaito finished his drink and Teague had still not touched a drop.

"You have a very suspicious nature Teague," the old man declared.

"I prefer the word inquisitive," explained Teague. "I like to know how things work. I'm not much of a fighter, I'm not very strong, but I understand strategy. There's a game father taught us. I'm pretty good at it."

"Then perhaps you could teach me," invited Kaito.

Teague got out his hand-carved set to explain the rules. There was a board made of wood marked out with a grid of dots joined by vertical, horizontal, and diagonal lines and the pieces were set up facing each other across this board on the dots. The pieces represented the different fighters on a battlefield. There were nine small round pieces of wood in front representing foot soldiers. A spear was carved on each piece. Behind them there were nine more pieces which were two charioteers, two horsemen, and two strange fortress pieces which Teague had never understood, because a fortress can't move. In the middle of the line were the Chief, the Mage, and the Chief's champion. The pieces were made from different types of wood: a pale creamy wood for one side and dark brown for the other.

Almost as soon as Teague began to explain the rules, it became clear that Kaito was familiar with the game and he produced, from a carved wooden box, an exquisite set made of stone and precious materials. The pieces were carved into elaborate figures with the tiniest detail. One set was mainly green stone with silver details, the other employed a dark rust red stone embellished with gold.

The board was a large square of glossy black stone inlaid with silver and gold lines. The Chiefs had torcs but wore them on their heads; Kaito said were called crowns. The Mages carried staffs topped with tiny red or green jewels according to their army. The horsemen had silver or gold spears, the chariots were wrought from silver or gold with tiny stone charioteers although, like Teague's more simple set, they also didn't have horses. Of most interest to Teague were the forts. Trethiwr had described a sort of fortress on the back of a giant animal, but they had settled for a simple circular piece with spikes around the top like the spikes around Ba-Dun. Kaito's pieces were elaborately carved elephants, with tiny ivory tusks and tiny sapphire eyes. On their backs were what looked like forts of silver and gold.

"Is this some sort of animal?" asked Teague. They were truly like nothing he had ever seen.

"They are called Haughti," explained Kaito.

Teague picked one up and examined the thing at the front.

"What's this?"

"It's called the trunk and it is like a nose and also an arm. They can pick up trees with it, and people."

"People?" asked Teague incredulously.

"The people train these animals to do their work for

them. They are so well trained that one can pick up a man and place him on its back. They are twice as tall as a big horse and ten times as heavy. Men ride on the Haughti's back to hunt the tiger, a giant wild cat, and to fight in battle. A great general, named Hannibal, used them against the Romani and defeated armies much larger than his own thanks to these amazing beasts."

"I don't believe it," said Teague simply.

"You will," declared Kaito. "They will form an important part of your future. But I thought we were going to play? You are full of questions."

Teague smiled and concentrated on the game. It didn't take long before he had set up a strong defensive position and captured several key pieces. Kaito then gave the game a little more attention but only succeeded in holding off the inevitable defeat for a little longer. To be fair, his mind was not really up to full speed first thing in the morning, while Teague was always either fully awake or fully asleep, never in between.

9

"You arrive at an important time," admitted Kaito. "You will share the rare privilege of witnessing the birth of a baby."

The boys looked around with some concern for a woman that they had not previously noticed.

"Come, outside," said Kaito, stepping out into the brisk fresh morning.

The air smelled sweet and heady after the heavy rainfall and, despite the deluge, the huge conical mound was still smouldering away as hot as ever.

"I'm sure it will be today," said Kaito, looking intently at the fire.

"What is it?" asked Teague nervously.

"Dragons," was Kaito's simple and somewhat unexpected reply.

The boys were stunned into silence. Even Teague could not form the many questions in his head into audible words. Dragons were talked about in stories but none of them had ever seen so much as a snake before.

As they watched there was a noticeable movement in the mound. The boys watched in stunned amazement as the first small red scaly head emerged from the top of the smoking pile of moss. It had bright orange eyes and two rows of tiny sharp spikes, which ran from the top of its head down its back. Its wings were leathery and moist, drying out as it stretched them in the glow of the embers. Then it took off briefly from the top of the pile and landed clumsily on the ground near to Blyth's feet. It stood only about six inches high and was very wobbly, but Blyth instinctively stepped back, well out of its way.

Another head emerged, followed by three more at varying intervals. Kaito fed several small scraps of meat to them and they all watched as the babies devoured their meal hungrily.

Teague found his voice at last, but all he could manage was,

"What… why… how… ?"

Kaito answered some of his unuttered questions with an explanation.

"Normally dragons take care of the eggs until they hatch and then care for the young for a short time afterwards until they can fend for themselves. But the mother of these babies had been causing problems for some time and she was killed by a warrior from north of here, where she had taken many head of cattle. I found her nest shortly afterwards and I've kept it hot to save the eggs. There should be as many as twenty or more but it looks as if these five are all that have survived."

"But why would you want to save dragons if they steal cattle?" asked Blyth.

"For many reasons."

"Such as?"

"For one, the world is not the sole preserve of people. Dragons are very beautiful creatures which have been around for as long as the mountains. They can also be very useful, both dead and alive. What right do I, or anyone else, have to destroy what may be the last surviving individuals of a breed?"

The old man paused and fixed his gaze at nothing in particular.

"They rarely attack people; they avoid us in fact. People go in search of them and kill them as trophies, bringing back just the head as proof of their brave deed. You have heard of warriors who claim the title 'Pen-Dragon'? Yet the head is of little value; the hide can be used to make a tough yet flexible protective material almost as strong as armour. Their blood may have healing properties, the claws will scratch the hardest stone, it is said the stomach can yield a cure for poison, and they may have many other uses. If we destroy them then we may never find out."

"How long will you look after them for?" asked Teague. He found their clumsy attempts to move and their tiny little squawks endearing, despite their fearsome appearance.

"They might hang around here for a few weeks and then they will just fly away. They live in the mountains mostly, to the north and west. They cannot be tamed, nor can they be trained, but they can choose to help people if they wish to, and occasionally one is enchanted by a very powerful Mage to protect some priceless treasure. They have a shared memory, and can communicate by thoughts alone. You will learn more about this in the future. Come, let's see to the horses and then get some food."

The boys' horses were lively and skittish, prancing from side to side trying to move away from the dragons, which spooked them. Kaito spoke softly to each in turn and they calmed down visibly. His own two horses were calm and relaxed as if they were setting an example to the newcomers. He then made sure they all had plenty of hay and poured some grain into the trough for them. He brushed each horse down in turn giving each boy a go on his own horse.

"You should always take personal care of your horse; it is your friend and your closest companion in battle. An animal is not a thing to be used and broken. It is a living creature with a soul which lives on to the next world. Imagine Lugh with no horses or hunting dogs. Imagine Bellenos or Dagda in a world with no birds or hares or geese or cockerels. The Gods even transform into animals. If you mistreat an animal you may be mistreating one of the Gods in disguise. These horses cannot feed themselves as long as we keep them tethered up. So we must feed them before we feed ourselves."

He finished brushing the last horse and gave it a comforting pat on the rump. Then he turned to the boys and suggested they might want something to eat now. Inside the hut he handed out some of the dense bread of the night before and gave each a large slab of rich reddish brown cured meat from a joint hanging from the roof. There was rich creamy butter made from goat's milk and some refreshing tea of Kaito's own creation. Teague reluctantly sipped a little of the tea this time; it smelled of chamomile and mint. It was pleasant enough but he left most of it and drank some water instead. When breakfast was mostly finished and all but Teague had finished their tea, Kaito settled down to telling them a story.

"Once many hundred ages ago, when our ancestors lived only in the fastness of the high mountains at the centre of the world, there was only one tribe. They were the ancestors of all the Keltoi. They were known as Eryri, the Eagle people. They were as strong and as tall as the mountains in which they lived, but they had not yet discovered the secret of fire and without fire they could not cook food, or smelt metal, or keep warm at night. They made weapons of stone and they hunted animals on the slopes of the mountain, eating the meat raw. They gathered berries and nuts and roots and seeds which they also ate uncooked. At night they wrapped themselves in the skins of the animals they had caught, and sheltered in caves, huddled together for warmth. When they tried to leave the mountains to find warmer lands and better food they found other people who had already discovered fire and had better weapons. These tribes had more food because they grew oats and barley and wheat as we do, and they kept animals in their villages as we do now. Because of this there were more of them and the Eryri were trapped in the mountains. At least there they were safe because they knew the land and because there was little that the other tribes wanted there.

"Then the bravest warrior of the Eryri, Rouduros, had a dream. In that dream he was visited by the great god Lugh, who told him to climb the highest mountain in the land and he would be rewarded. The highest mountain was sacred to the God Poeninos. Its slopes were white with snow from Samonios to Samonios, and its peak was so high that it scraped the sky and tore the clouds to ribbons.

"At the next new moon, as the day began with the setting of the sun, he made a sacrifice to Lugh to ask for a successful journey and to Poeninos for safe passage on the mountain. At sunrise on the same day he set out to climb the mountain. When he reached almost to the very top of the mountain he found a deep cleft in the rock, in front of a wide ledge. His fingers and feet were so cold he could not feel them at all. Frost formed on

85

his moustache; little icicles hung from the tips. He was tired, and frozen to the core, and was having trouble breathing. As he approached the cave he staggered and fell face down in the snow. Bellenos was, even then, already retreating below the jagged horizon and the sky was growing dark as the new day began. He knew if he stayed there that he would surely die, and yet he had not the strength or the will to pull himself up. He uttered a faint plea to Poeninos of the high mountains and Lugh, protector of travellers, and then the darkness of the new day and the darkness of the other-world overcame him and he slept. As he slept he dreamed that Lugh, the shining one, came and stood over him, glowing ever brighter. Rouduros could feel the warmth radiating from the God and he felt himself lifted up and lain out on a dry rock. Lugh stayed by his side, burning as bright as the Belotenios fires, turning night to day. In the morning when Bellenos returned Rouduros awoke, but of Lugh there was no sign. Instead there was a dragon with huge yellow eyes, watching him and radiating warmth. Rouduros had two thoughts at once. On one hand he felt terror at being helpless, faced with the dragon, on the other he realised that it was the dragon which had saved him from certain death. His body shook with an involuntary movement before he calmed himself.

"'You need have no fear, if I wished to harm you there was plenty of time through the night.' The words of the dragon entered his head as thoughts, not sounds.

'Thank you, and thank the Gods, you saved me.'

'It is of no consequence. It cost me nothing to help you but would have cost you everything if I had not.'

'Well I thank you anyway.'

'Why did you come here, human?' the dragon enquired.

Rouduros explained about the dream.

'You have been brave, and fortunate, but you seem troubled. Your people suffer, you seek to help them and risk your own life to do so. You fear me but you fear failure more. I can help you.'

"Just after sunset at the beginning of the next day Rouduros sat on the dragon's back as if he was riding a horse; a horse with wings, and shiny red scales the colour of glowing coals, and huge yellow eyes like a cat's, but with more intelligence. The beast lifted itself up and opened its wings out. They were like two vast ship's sails unfurling, dark, reddish brown, and leathery, with a claw on the leading edge, just like the little 'night-flying-mouse' that lives in trees, but vastly bigger.

"The dragon leapt off the ledge and dropped some way before the wind caught under its wings and with a few lazy flaps and twists it soared out over the land towards the tree line, where it landed.

"'Pick up sticks, and broken branches; make a pile. There, on that large flat rock; it is ideal.'

"Rouduros did as he was told and after a while there was a huge pile of wood, as high as Rouduros himself, on the great slab of rock. Then the dragon breathed a tongue of fire onto the pile and it began to burn fiercely. The flames lit up the night and warmed the warrior. The light sparkled in his eyes and many villagers came to see what was happening. The dragon saw the people coming up the hillside and he opened his great wings and took off in the opposite direction before they arrived. Only Rouduros had seen the dragon and he told the story which was passed down to every generation.

"Once the Eryri had the use of fire they learned how to cook food and smelt copper and tin, to make bronze weapons and farming tools, they could keep warm at night and keep wild animals away. Every family kept a fire burning in their own hearth and if anyone's fire went out they could always get it from another hearth. After many ages their numbers grew. They learned how to smelt iron - cheaper than bronze - which meant that every warrior could have a strong sword. Soon they were able to challenge the tribes of the plains and spread out across all the land: East to the far mountains, and West to the great western ocean, South to the southern sea and North to our own island of Pretan.

"But some people forgot the story and sometimes people saw the dragon's breath at the top of the mountain. Once in a while a sheep or goat would go missing from the mountainside and soon the people of the mountains began to blame a dragon, which they said lived near the top of the mountain. It was a descendant of Rouduros who was selected to kill the dragon. He climbed the great mountain and, with the help of his iron sword and bronze shield, he slew the dragon. There were a clutch of young dragons huddled at the back of the cave and he slew these as well. All except one, which escaped and flew from the mountain and was never seen again.

"Dragons live for hundreds, maybe thousands, of years and only produce one or two clutches of eggs in a lifetime. Like humans they have long memories and the stories are passed on to each generation. Unlike humans they are not vengeful or vindictive, but never again will dragons trust humans as that dragon trusted Rouduros. The most you can hope for is that if you show a dragon kindness it may be repaid; something you would do well to remember."

10

Over the next few weeks, Kaito began to teach them some basic magic as well as imparting his philosophy on life, padding it all out with humorous stories, snippets of general knowledge, and potted histories of the clan, the tribe, and the world beyond. He taught them about plant extracts and their properties. They made a painkiller from birch and beech bark, and a sleep-inducing drink using ingredients such as chamomile, grown locally; lemon balm, from the shores of the southern sea; and a rare herb which Kaito insisted came from beyond the western sea at the edge of the world. This was the drink he gave to Blyth on their first night. They learned how to make Kaito's morning tea, which could contain up to nine ingredients including a black powder and some small green leaves which Kaito said were from the same plant and came from the farthest eastern edge of the world, along with a hard root which had to be cut finely, a common local plant with small yellow flowers and long finger shaped leaves, and some pinkish nuts and tiny brown rods of compressed powder which Kaito again insisted came from beyond the western ocean, which Blyth presumed meant they came from the land of the Gods. They learned Kaito's almost divine ability to control horses with a whisper and a look. They learned to create the same sort of fire that burned night and day in Kaito's fireplace, with barely any attention, and they learned how to create the unique waterproofing charm that Kaito used to make his roundhouse so warm and dry. Kaito showed them his wax tablet and they watched him write a message to Epona which then turned into her reply from far away in the east of Pretan. Kaito had to read it for them as they were still learning to interpret the symbols that Kaito used. Indeed writing was something alien to all Keltoi, with the exception of Mages, and this was what they would spend most of the next few months learning.

At Ba-Dun the death of the Mage had left a vacuum, of power and understanding, among the clan. Most people agreed that Darruwen had not been right in his interpretation of events. His death at the hands of the Gods was clear evidence of this. Not everyone agreed that Trethiwr was either, but nobody had any answers about what to do now. Into this void came a traveller from across the sea with a mysterious air of confidence. He arrived one wet and windy evening less than a week after Darruwen's death. The Mage's body had been burned on a vast pyre a few days earlier but nobody was able to finish the rites so the charred remains lay in a pile of wind-blown ash. The next morning dawned bright and fresh and the stranger went out of the fortress and conducted a suitable ceremony which satisfied everyone that he was a Mage. Urien formally invited him to take over the vacant position and he agreed, taking up residence in Darruwen's hut and speaking with all of the villagers in turn, at length, over the next few weeks.

The new Mage was a Deru-Weido, named Golow-Vur, and he interpreted correctly that there would be a shortage of food this year with all the bad weather that had already gone before. Since it was clear there was bad feeling between Ba-Dun and Maywr-Dun he encouraged an attack against the larger fortress. Cuilleana however implored him to consider her daughter, Rhuthgem, and the other hostages. He considered this for a few days, until he came up with a plan to rescue the hostages.

He travelled alone to Maywr-Dun and spent some time watching the fortress from a distance. He built a hide in the edge of dense woods, as close to the main gate as he could get, and lived off his wits and a little magic. The gates were left open during the day but there was always at least one warrior there, observing who went in or out. Hunters came and went as well as farmers and merchants. The defences were kept in reasonable repair although there may not have been as much ammunition stockpiled around the walls as in more troubled times.

After observing the comings and goings for three days he had chosen his target. He selected a warrior who was clearly of high status, judging by his large golden torc, and low intelligence, from the fact that he killed a small boar just three paces from Golow-Vur's hide but did not notice the structure. As the warrior trussed the boar to a pole for transporting back to the fortress, the Deru-Weido emerged silently from the hide behind him. Holding his staff high, he cast a spell which produced a cloud of smoke, and he spoke to the warrior in a calm and level voice.

"Turn around," he commanded.

The warrior whirled around and faced a cloud of smoke from which emerged an imposing figure wearing long undyed robes and holding an oak staff in his left hand and a small glittering jewel, suspended from a golden chain, in his right hand.

The jewel spun and caught the light as effectively as it caught the warrior's attention and the wizard spoke soft words which lulled his target into a subliminal sleep. While in this state Golow-Vur gave him instructions.

"You will persuade the gatekeeper to come hunting with you tomorrow," he intoned. "Bring him here to this place so that I may speak with him."

"I will my lord," said the warrior in a flat monotone voice.

"Go then," said the mage

The next day the warrior brought the gatekeeper to Golow-Vur, who placed him under the same spell. He commanded that the two should arrange for the prisoners to be brought out of the castle the next day, just before sunrise.

The next morning, as he had ordered, the nine bewildered hostages from Ba-Dun were herded out of the great fortress by the warrior and allowed to pass by the gatekeeper as if on the order of their own Chief. A few early risers said nothing, as the two were high status so would not be questioned except, perhaps, by the Chief or one of the Mages. As soon as they were with Golow-Vur he led them as far away from the fortress as possible and headed back for Ba-Dun. They had no horses, as Golow-Vur had decided it would attract too much attention if they had, so they walked all the way, which meant they did not arrive back in Ba-Dun until late in the evening. A feast was arranged by the village, at short notice, to celebrate the return of their family and friends. Much good food was eaten, and a great deal of mead and wine was drunk.

Golow-Vur concentrated on his next plans. He knew they could not mount a direct assault on Maywr-Dun but he needed to control the most powerful castle in the region in order to control the tribe itself. He decided on stealth and guerrilla tactics to draw out the warriors into open battle, and to use his magic skills to secure a victory for his adopted clan. Then he could take over the whole region.

The next day Ba-Dun was still asleep following the previous night's celebrations when, around mid-morning, Kano-Walo brought the fight to Ba-Dun. He was incensed about the brazen way in which his hostages had somehow managed to walk unchallenged out of the fortress. The gatekeeper had no memory of events and was sick with fever and headache. One of the Chief's nephews, a strong but somewhat thick-headed warrior, was also ill and nothing he said made any sense.

At dawn Kano-Walo left Maywr-Dun with five hundred of his best warriors, chariots, horses, and his three Mages. A hundred wagons followed with supplies of corn, cattle, sheep, and several hundred servants and family members to provide support. He intended to capture Ba-Dun and control it fully, once and for all. The warriors quickly stole several score of cattle and sheep which had been grazing in the fields. There had been peace in the region for so long that people were out of the habit of taking proper precautions. They did not set fire to the crops as Kanvodur had prophesied that food would be scarce this year. They burned some of the peasants' huts which huddled in clusters around the outside of the village. The occupants ran screaming from the flames, most in nothing but a tunic, a few naked. One angry farmer who felt he had nothing left to live for attacked the nearest mounted warrior with a bronze sickle that hung from the rafters of his rapidly-burning hut. He was struck down without a second thought and his head was impaled on a spear and hurled over the walls of Ba-Dun as a first warning shot.

Inside the village, after the previous night's drinking, weary warriors with aching heads struggled to gather the will to defend their fortress and tripped over each other in a mad scramble for spears and shields and swords. Horses were brought by harried grooms and the whole village was a mass of frenzied yet pained activity. Only Golow-Vur was calm and level headed. As soon as he realized that an attack was being made, he went straight to his hut. Here he filled a large jar with a potion which he had been brewing, over a constantly burning flame, and headed out to the central clearing. He called one warrior at a time to him and bade them each take a drink. The potion had a rapid effect, soothing aching heads and filling each warrior with renewed energy. It contained a number of ingredients but the most potent of all was a white powder which gave the user strength and immunity to pain, as well as keeping them wide awake, heightening the senses and speeding up thought processes.

As each warrior took their dose they became noticeably more efficient in their preparations. Then, under the leadership of Kyndyrn, a force rode out of the village to confront the invaders. Just one hundred mounted men and women and fifty chariots left the fortress, against the five hundred warriors from Maywr-Dun. Bristling spears glinted in the sunlight as the attacking force grouped together to face Kyndyrn's first attack. His head was clear now but he did not feel the need to hurry, and he began to beat his shield with his sword to intimidate the enemy. The rest of the warriors joined in, adding fierce battle cries to the already terrible din.

The army of Maywr-Dun stood firm however, as Siaradur encouraged them with well-chosen rhetoric. Then Kyndyrn ordered the chariots forward, charging headlong for the array of spears. They stopped, inches from the spear tips, turning as the warriors leapt from them, swords slashing, to come down amongst the front lines. Some were skewered like meat for the fire but many more landed on their feet, hewing the enemy with a skill and strength which seemed to come from the Gods. The charioteers retreated a short distance as the warriors broke down the first line of defence. Then Kyndyrn led the mounted warriors into the fray and the enemy were routed. Kano-Walo stood firm, surrounded by his best warriors, but the rest of his army melted away along with his Mages, who ran at the first sign of defeat. Into this scene came the Deru-Weido, Golow-Vur, who quickly took control. With a wave of his staff, and several carefully chosen words, he cast a spell of calming over the whole scene, trying to keep the bloodshed to a minimum. He needed the Chief and his cohort alive to serve his plans. He ordered the warriors on both sides to sheath their weapons and dismount from their horses. Urien arrived with a reserve force but Golow-Vur persuaded him that the battle was over and there was more important business to discuss, such as who would become Chief of all the tribe.

In the following months Urien moved himself and his family and close retinue to Maywr-Dun, where Kano-Walo was permitted to remain as a substantial landowner, after swearing the triple oath of allegiance to Urien. Golow-Vur took control of religion over the whole region and appointed Deru-Weidi to all the villages and forts in turn. Kyndyrn became the head of Ba-Dun but swore the triple oath of absolute allegiance to Urien as did all the other clan leaders. By Samonios, the New Year and beginning of winter, Golow-Vur had complete control over all the Dwr-Y-Tryges through his network of Deru-Weidi Mages.

It was early in June of that same year that Kaito told the boys he had taught them as much as he could for now, and that they would have to go to study with the Deru-Weidi. They could have travelled north across the wide river through the lands of the Silures and over the mountains of the Ordovici to Ynis-Mona; many young students were sent here from the mainland. Kaito, however, wanted the boys to go to the place where their father had trained, and so they packed their things ready for a long journey across the sea, and south to Lugh-Dun.

11

The boys took their horses and packs the next morning and headed for the coast, not far from the mint, which produced the coins for the Dwr-Y-Tryges. There was a busy port taking tin, copper, iron, cattle, wool, grain, and hunting dogs to Armorica and on to Rome, and bringing back silks, wine, herbs and spices, some pottery, and gold. They persuaded the reluctant owner of one of the larger trading vessels to take them across the sea with their three horses, in exchange for one of Blyth's arm torcs, which was of almost pure gold, and a small purse full of Dwr-Y-Tryges currency. They would be meeting their guide, a woman named Gwenn, at the port in Unellia.

The crossing was uneventful, the horses placid under the hypnotic mind control of the boys who took turns to stay with them. The boat owner said he had never seen horses so well behaved on a boat before.

Abbon got a bit seasick towards the end of the journey but Blyth brewed him up some sleeping drink and he slept soundly for the rest of the journey.

At the port the boys looked for Gwenn. They found her very quickly as she stood taller than almost every other man or woman in the busy port. Her hair was thick, yet so pale it almost pure white, and fell to below her waist. She had arranged for a place to stay for the night before continuing on to Lugh-Dun which was six days' ride away. The boys ate well on roast boar, and drank watered-down wine, before sleeping deeply in a small hut near the edge of the port.

The next day dawned bright and very windy. The boys set off with Gwenn, leaving behind the busy port, bustling and smelly, and plunging into dense woodland and the sweet smell of spring flowers and new green leaves. Gwenn's horse was white, with a long flowing mane; Blyth considered it amusing how often horses were like their owners, but this was an extreme example. It was the largest stallion he had ever seen, taller and more powerful than any in Ba-Dun, he was sure. Unlike most white horses it was completely white all over, even its skin was pale; there was almost no darkening around the nose and mouth. Gwenn also had the palest skin he had ever seen. The horse's mane was very long and flowing, and Gwenn paid it extra special attention when grooming, as she did her own long flowing hair. Lastly the eyes; both horse and rider had piercing blue eyes that looked like a hillside lake on a sunny day, when the sky reflects in the deep still cold water and you feel like you are looking straight into the land of the Gods.

They reached Cosedia, the Chief city of the Unelli, an easy day's ride from the port. By comparison to Ba-Dun this was a city. Unlike the Dwr-Y-Tryges the Unelli, like most tribes of the Galli, were a united people with a supreme Chief over all the tribe. The Chief, advised by the Deru-Weidi, dispensed justice and presided over all aspects of life over the whole region. His most important function was however to raise and maintain a large army of warriors who would defend the tribe against enemies and would protect the farmers, and traders, and craftspeople from attack, either by bandits, or from invaders. When times were hard they might go on a raid to steal cattle or sheep from neighbouring tribes.

The town must have held several thousand people: there were huts built from stone; a great long house, bigger than any the boys had seen, where warriors gathered for feasting; a marketplace where all sorts of goods from far and near were either bartered, or sold for the little gold and silver coins with a picture of Bellenos on one side and a hunting chariot on the other. Gwenn took them to a secret place where the Deru-Weidi gathered to conduct ceremonies, a grove of ancient oak trees in the forest near to the town. She explained how the oak was sacred to them and showed them some of the local plants which had medicinal value.

They stayed in a large hut which was set aside specifically for the purpose of travellers as there were a great many merchants and officials that passed through the town. The next day they continued on to Suindinum which was the Chief town of the Cenomanni; this was similar to Cosedia and the boys began to get an idea of just how big the world was and how small and fragmented their own tribe seemed in comparison. When, on the third day, they arrived in Genabo on the Liger River they were blasé about the busy marketplace, with the rows of huts, all open on one side, displaying every conceivable luxury. There were fresh fish from the fast cold river, pots of every shape and size, from tiny little apothecary bottles to great big jars for oil or wheat. There was wine, and oil, and fresh fruits such as apples, which were familiar, and peaches, which were new to them. The blacksmith had on display a number of swords as well as more domestic items such as scythes, horseshoes, and ploughs.

Farmers were selling surplus crops, and there were a few horses for sale which were attracting a lot of attention from a small group of Carnuti warriors, their shields embossed with bronze and each showing the same insignia denoting loyalty to their Chief. One of the warriors tried to mount the largest horse, a roan stallion, but the horse was barely broken and showed a certain reluctance to accept a rider. It bucked as the warrior was still mounting and he waved goodbye to his dignity. Then another warrior, attempting to show him how a horse should be ridden, leapt swiftly onto the stallion's back. The big roan stood still for a moment but, just as the warrior thought she had made a good impression, the horse twisted and bucked, sending her over its shoulders and depositing her in an unceremonious bundle of bruises on the floor.

The rest of the warriors broke down in fits of laughter at their comrade's embarrassment but that made her all the more determined to mount the horse and show it, and them, who was boss. She drew her sword and gave the horse a swift slap with the flat of the blade, amid cries of fury from the horse's owner. The animal raced off at top speed through the crowded market, knocking over piles of fruit and vegetables; people dived for cover in every direction. Frightened and furious, it careered straight towards the boys, and Gwenn. As fast as she could, Gwenn grabbed at Abbon and Teague, dragging them out of the path of the thundering hooves, only to look back and realize that Blyth was standing dead still, right in front of it. Time seemed to slow as she threw the two younger boys into a large hut and tried to turn back for Blyth. He seemed to be whispering something to the horse, which surely could not hear him, as it whinnied furiously and reared up in front of him. Its front hooves whirled like scythes on a cloudy autumn day, just inches from his face, and yet he did not move a muscle, nor even blink an eye. Even as Gwenn watched, the horse calmed down and stood in front of Blyth as if nothing had happened.

Then, as if that was not enough, it turned and allowed Blyth to mount it without protest. Blyth turned the horse to where the astonished warriors stood. The owner, who had been berating the warrior for striking his horse, simply stared with his mouth open. Gwenn was suitably impressed as well, although she at least knew where Blyth's power over the horse came from.

"Kaito has taught you well," was all she said.

The horse trader came over to where they stood. He began stroking and patting the beautiful beast's velvety neck, and he looked up at Blyth.

"How old are you?" he asked.

Blyth hesitated, as the way the man spoke was so different from what he was used to. The words were almost the same but the pronunciation rendered them hard to understand. "I am fourteen at the next moon," he replied, hoping he could be understood well enough.

The trader seemed to understand because he muttered incredulously to himself, "Still a boy but with the skills of a God." And then more directly, to Blyth, "Are you a warrior?"

"No sir," said Blyth.

"You should be. We need people who can control horses as you can. We need the Gods to help us in the south beyond Lugh-Dun. Our own people divided: either allies or slaves of the Romani. Chiefs sold their brothers in exchange for grand houses such as would befit Lugh or Deus Pater. But the wealth they enjoy in this life will not last. The Romani give with one hand

and take away with the other: taxes and slaves and unfair trades, people forced to join their army and fight in far off places, for what? A promise of more wealth if they live to tell the tale. But what of the Gods, what of the next life, the one that matters? What of freedom? A wild plant, a wild animal, precious metals in the ground, a river, a tree, a sunset; these things don't belong to any one person. They are the property of all, for all to share. Whoever kills the boar owns the boar, who farms the land owns the land, who pans the gold owns the gold. Now the Romani say parts of the forest belong to certain important people, that lands which are not being farmed belong to them and that gold in the ground belongs to them. Where will it end?"

Blyth had understood about every other word and could not think of a reply.

Gwenn spoke softly in the local dialect, "We seek to preserve the ways of our people, but these boys will help in other ways than as warriors. The Gods have a purpose for them."

The horse trader observed her properly, for the first time, and realized that she must be a Deru-Weido. He apologized very humbly; to offend the Deru-Weidi was not something that even a high Chief would dare to do. They had several curses, but the worst of these was exclusion: they would exclude a person from all sacrifices and religious festivals, which meant they could not enter the next life. Others would avoid them for fear of being infected by this curse, which meant that they could not trade or deal with other people. They became outcast; if someone did them a wrong they could not seek help from the law because that was dispensed, ultimately, by the Deru-Weidi.

He turned to Blyth.

"Please take the horse as my gift to you, young man. He has the wildest spirit I have ever seen, in all my years of dealing with horses. I don't think anybody else could ever hope to control him as you have done."

They set out early the next day for the long ride to Nevez-Dun. Blyth rode his new horse, which meant that they had a spare horse to carry most of the packs; this was handy as the ride was longer and more difficult than it had been on previous days. Nevez-Dun was another large and bustling town, but they had little time to enjoy it, arriving late in the day. The following day they had a shorter ride to Bibracte, chief city of the Aedui, their last stopover before Lugh-Dun. The influence of Roman life was stronger here than anywhere else they had been so far. In the marketplace, Gwenn paid for some food with a gold coin showing the head of Bellenos on one side and a stylized charioteer on the other; these symbols were familiar to the boys from the coins of the Dwr-Y-Tryges, although the quality was better. The vendor gave her a few silver and bronze coins, some of which bore a different head; Gwenn told them it was the Roman sun God, Apollo. On the other side was a very clear image of a chariot pulled by four horses, side by side: a quadriga. One coin showed a picture of Dumnoreix, a tribal Chief, with a picture of a boar, the symbol of the Aedui, on the reverse. The houses were different here as well; there were still a few wattle and daub huts but the further south they travelled the more there appeared large houses with regular straight walls, and roofs not of thatch but with a kind of flat red or green coloured pottery. All this was new to Blyth, Teague, and Abbon, who gazed in wonder at the huge number of buildings with two floors and enclosed courtyards. There were several springs and special channels which delivered water to all parts of the city, as well as creating displays of falling water.

The last day of riding took them to their destination of Lugh-Dun however they did not enter the city itself. Gwenn took them straight to a place outside the city where there was a large grove of oak trees, regularly spaced in two rows joined at one end by a wide arc. Gwenn showed them several simple huts arranged nearby where, she explained, they would be sleeping. Compared to some of the large ornate houses they had seen on their journey, these were very simple. In fact, they were no different to the huts they were used to back in Ba-Dun. Blyth was the first to comment, as he so often was.

"I thought we would be living in some big brick house with a tiled roof and a garden like we saw in Bibracte," he declared, somewhat outraged.

"You are here to learn, not to relax," Gwenn

informed them. "You won't need comfort here. You will barely get to see your beds. It's late," she added, "get some sleep now; you will be up early."

It was still light outside but then again it was the longest day of the year, so it would hardly get dark before sunrise. Blyth and Teague brewed some sleep tea. Teague was asleep before it was brewed; Abbon fell asleep after the first sip. Blyth drank his and Teague's and most of Abbon's before he too fell into a deep sleep.

12

Teague woke with the first rays of the sun and brewed some morning tea for Blyth. He didn't have all the ingredients he needed but he did the best he could. Gwenn arrived just as it was ready and was surprised to see Teague awake. She prodded the other two with an oak staff topped with a polished blue stone that gleamed in the early morning light, and told them to wake up. Blyth stirred irritably. Abbon rolled over, trying to avoid the prodding.

Gwenn persisted until Blyth tried to grab the staff. She pulled back and he was dragged a few feet across the hard earth floor. He sat up and glared at her, then remembered where he was. With an effort he calmed down, and Teague handed him a drink.

"Lessons begin today," Gwenn informed them. "The time for childish games is over, for all of you, not just for Blyth. You have much to learn. Get ready, and come to the grove as soon as you are."

The boys drank the tea, pulled on their brachii - it was too warm for anything else - and headed for the grove. The great gnarled oaks towered above their heads, reaching for the sky. The dense green foliage providing shade in the otherwise oppressive heat of mid-summer. They swore the triple oath over sacred oak boughs, swearing to keep all that they learned secret. A lamb was sacrificed and their teacher examined the entrails to ensure that none swore falsely.

The lessons turned out to be very dull and consisted of learning endless poems and stories. They told of the beginning of the world, of Deus-Pater, the sky father who created the world, beginning with night and winter; of Bellenos the fire God who came next and created the day and the summer. Then of Lugh; gifted in all arts, protector of merchants and travellers, messenger of the Gods. Lugh was one of many triple Gods; the boys grappled with the concept of a being which was Tri-Oino: three in one. Blyth seemed determined not to understand and kept bringing it back to the question 'how can anything be both three beings and yet one at the same time?' Gwenn helped a little with a plant she found growing abundantly on the forest floor. The flowers were small purple trumpets with five petals but it was the leaves she gave to each of the boys and showed them how they had three distinct parts and yet were clearly one leaf. Blyth finally appeared to accept the idea but was perhaps just worn down by the persistence of the teachers.

They stopped for lunch, which was always a simple meal of bread and wine, and the work continued through the sweltering hot summer afternoon. The lessons were dull and on one occasion Teague was sent to find a quiet place and practice reciting a poem about Cernunnos. A little later, Gwenn found him fast asleep under a beech tree, a little way from the oak grove. He received three strokes with a birch stick to remind him of the importance of concentrating on his studies. He bit back tears, for fear of being teased by the others, but from then on he always kept some morning tea in a small skin bottle in case he needed a boost.

The boys went to bed at sunset and woke at sunrise every day, except on the new moon and the full moon, when they were allowed a rest day. Food was simple, consisting of dense seedy bread, milk, butter, wine or ale mixed with water, with root vegetables, nuts and berries as they came into season, and meat only in the evening on alternate days.

The lessons included finding out about all the plants that had medicinal or magical properties and learning to identify each plant and its uses. They began to learn about the secret letters used by the Deru-Weidi, which could be spelled out on the fingers of the hand as well as written down, but they were told that the Deru-Weidi did not write down their stories or secrets in case they fell into the wrong hands. Writing was only used to communicate where no other method was available and then the writing should be destroyed after it had served its purpose. This meant that huge amounts of information had to be committed to memory, which could be tedious for the children. Much of it was written in poetry but still it was a lot to learn and would take years.

One long hot summer afternoon Abbon became restless and decided to have a bit of fun. He was supposed to practice reciting the story of Epona, the Goddess after whom his mother was named. She could ride better than all the Gods and she oversaw the breeding of horses, as well as having influence on wheat crops and fertility. She could also turn into a horse at will and Abbon wondered what animal he would like to turn into if he could. He thought about being a squirrel as he was so good at climbing trees; as he thought about this it seemed natural to see if he could climb one of the great oaks. He glanced across to see if Gwenn or any of the other teachers or students were looking his way and then disappeared behind the trunk of one of the largest and most gnarled of the sacred trees. The bole must have been more than twenty paces around and the first branch was at least three times the height of Abbon, but the trunk was knobbly and scarred in places and it was only a matter of minutes before Abbon was high in the canopy, looking down on his brothers and Gwenn. He rested for a while in the cool shade, lying full length along one of the tree's huge limbs, but Abbon could not sit still for long without thinking of more devious activities. He managed to reach some small, developing acorns and pulled them off. Taking careful aim he hit Blyth with one and then Teague with a second. He also fired one off at a girl who annoyed him because she had been the best and quickest at learning everything so far. She blamed first Teague then Blyth, but the boys both guessed the source of the trouble and started searching the trees above them for their little brother. Gwenn came over to see what was causing the disturbance and followed Blyth's gaze into the ceiling of green. She spelled some secret words on her hands and pointed her staff in the general direction of the trees. There was a swish of sound and a shimmer in the air, the branches shook and Abbon fell onto the leaf-strewn grass at her feet. He groaned but managed not to cry in front of everybody. Gwenn picked him up and handed him to one of the more stern teachers who took him away to explain a bit more about the sacred oak. The explanation was accompanied by a series of sharp blows on the palm with a birch stick; they left a red mark across his palm that lasted for a few days. It made little difference, because Abbon just could not help causing trouble whenever he got bored.

But Abbon's streak of mischief was a minor inconvenience to the Deru-Weidi teachers compared with Blyth's lack of emotional control. When things were going well for him he could be cool and calm, such as when he stared down the raging stallion in Genabo, but if anything didn't go his way or if he thought he was being unfairly treated he would become uncontrollable and would take a long time to calm down. He was reciting a poem about different types of wood and their uses when the teacher corrected him on a minor point. Blyth got so angry he threw his staff at the teacher and stormed off into the woods. Gwenn found him but could not persuade him to return with her. Eventually she had to pick him up bodily and carry him kicking and screaming back to the huts. She threw him into the boys hut and cast a spell over the entrance. Later he was given nine strikes with a birch stick, which simply made him more angry, and then left back in the hut until he had calmed down enough to be let out.

This behaviour occurred once or twice a week in one form or another and the teachers all complained that he was not the right material for the Deru-Weidi, and swore they would refuse to teach him. Gwenn, alone, argued for him to remain and insisted that his destiny was tied in with the Deru-Weidi and all the tribes of the Keltoi. She stood taller than her peers and her white mane of hair swished as she turned from one to another, reminding them how his father had been of a similar character but had become a great wizard in his time. (She omitted the part about him being thrown out of the school before finishing his studies!) She herself had trained with Trethiwr and remembered how he had been quite a handful but had eventually learned to control his temper while travelling.

They agreed, grudgingly, to give Blyth a bit more

time to grow up, although he was now a man at fourteen, so he continued with his studies. Lughunasath followed Belotenios, and Samonios followed Lughunasath. The tantrums did die down a little. Perhaps as the days grew shorter and the nights longer he was getting more sleep, perhaps he feared the birch stick across the hand, or maybe he was just growing up a bit.

During the depths of winter, lessons were much shorter and consisted mainly of revision. Food and other supplies came from Lugh-Dun on a regular basis, unless the roads became impassable. A great deal of time was spent sitting around roaring fires, glittering with green flames, telling stories and working on crafts.

Towards the end of winter, plans were made for the great feast of Imbolc. On the eve of the great feast, a bitterly cold and crisp evening with flakes of snow flurrying around. Blyth had been collecting firewood, as he had been doing a year ago when he first met his great-grandfather. He had been preoccupied with memories of his father, who had come home shortly after that meeting. His mind had wandered from there to his mother leaving, and his father being dragged away to be killed, of the brothers' flight from the village on that terrible night and their long voyage to this place. As a result he had not paid much attention to his collecting and had returned not long after dark with his load. Another student commented that he had not brought back very much and Blyth had immediately become angry, feeling that anyone should know this was a difficult time for him.

"You don't understand how I feel!" he screamed. "Nobody does."

"I was only saying there wasn't that much wood there; it doesn't matter you know."

A few people came over to try and reason with Blyth but the more they tried to calm him down the angrier he got until, seeing his wild-eyed stallion tethered to a pole nearby, he decided that he only really had one friend in the whole world and it was that horse. He untied him, mounted up and rode straight through the babble of people gathered around him and off into the woods.

Somehow this felt right to him. It reminded him of their desperate search for Kaito's hut in the driving rain and lightning of that terrible night nearly a year before. The difference this time was that he was on his own, and he did not have the slightest idea where to go. He needed to get away, as far away as possible, from all the stupid people trying to force him to learn stupid stories. For what? To fulfil some dubious prophesy. He knew a thing or two now about surviving, he knew some magic and how to brew potions, he had a knife and he could start a fire easily enough; Kaito had taught him that. He thought he could probably make a shelter and waterproof it with a magic charm. Lugh-Dun was to the West, Bibracte to the North, and steep mountains to the East. He decided to ride south, following the river downstream. Gwenn had ridden after him immediately but even her horse was no match for the great roan stallion with the fire in his eyes and the wild still in his blood.

Blyth rode, blindly, as the snow began to fall more heavily and blew around in little flurries through the thin trees. The cold stabbed through his cloak and bit into him as he rode on, driven by pure anger. He rode through the night, his horse showing no sign of tiredness, although he was becoming stiff and slow with cold. As the dawn came up he was already over one hundred thousand paces to the south. Hypothermia and tiredness were affecting his judgement, although it was warmer here so far south, and despite desperately needing to rest and get warm by a fire he decided to carry on. Shadows formed into solid objects in his exhausted mind. He ducked to avoid non-existent branches and then crashed through real ones which he had failed to notice. He thought he sensed someone following him although in fact Gwenn was more than a thousand paces behind him, following his trail. In the dark recesses of his faltering mind he sensed the need to stop and make camp but, even while he was looking for a suitable place, he finally passed out and slid limply from the back of his horse.

13

His faithful steed stood over him, protective and loyal. Blyth lay, where he fell, for several hours. At dusk a squad of eight Roman soldiers, a contubernium, passed by, returning to their legion at Narbo.

The Decanus, Lucius Sulpicius Longus, third son of a wealthy landowner, had joined the army out of patriotic fervour and hoped, perhaps, to win some land for himself one day. He ordered two men to investigate. As they approached the horse it stamped and whinnied frantically before finally retreating to avoid capture. The men lifted Blyth's limp and freezing body and carried him back to the patrol. Lucius searched Blyth's lifeless form for any sign of wealth or importance. Finding nothing, no weapons except for a small knife, no torc or other valuables, no staff or amulets, he declared, "Just a common Gaul, of no importance." And then as an afterthought, "Yet why such a magnificent horse?"

The stallion remained a short distance away watching his master, waiting.

The Decanus ordered three of his men to catch the horse, and another two to go and fetch water from the river. The two servants made a fire and Blyth was laid nearby. The two soldiers returned with water, which was set to warm over the fire. Meanwhile the three legionaries attempting to catch the wild stallion were making no progress, but were providing much amusement for the remainder. They had tried simply coaxing the horse and offering food, a futile act since grass grew abundantly here anyway. It was dark now, and they had fallen over a number of times.

Eventually the Decanus told them to leave it. The horse seemed unwilling to leave its master who was beginning to show signs of life now.

"Quisnam es tu?" Lucius asked.

Blyth looked up through drooping eyelids. A man was speaking but not words, just strange sounds. He closed his eyes and his head dropped back to the ground.

The Decanus tried again, "Salve," he said.

Blyth tried to speak, but what he mumbled was no more intelligible than the soldier's ramblings so he gave up again.

"Servius!" The Decanus called one of the servants.

"Try talking to him in your Gallic," he ordered.

Servius was the son of a carpenter who was Salluvi by birth. He was enslaved, but later freed when his master died, so Servius was born a freeman, but his father had always held on to his roots and made sure Servius could speak both Gallic and Latin. As soon as the law had been changed to allow plebeians to join the army he had enlisted, seeking an opportunity to acquire some land. Ironically his legion was now based close to his father's old home.

"Hi, I'm Severix," he said, using the Gallic variant of his name which his father often used. "What's your name?"

"Blyth."

"Blyth eh? Where are you from?"

"Pretan."

"He says he's from Albion," Servius translated. "His name is Blyth, which means wolf."

"What is his business here?"

"Why are you here?"

"I got lost."

"Lost? It's more than lost when you have crossed the sea and ridden for many thousand paces!"

Blyth thought it best not to say any more. He had heard that the Romani did not like the Deru-Weidi. In fact he had heard nothing but bad things about the Romani and he wasn't about to help them in any way.

"Ask him why he is here, so far from home," ordered Lucius.

"I did; he won't say."

The Decanus thought briefly but decided to play it cool until he had the horse.

"Persuade him to call his horse," he ordered quietly.

"We need to groom your horse, and feed it. It won't come to us," said Servius.

Blyth looked across to where the magnificent stallion stood, about fifty paces away, nervous and jumpy.

"Go!" he shouted. "Run away."

The beast hesitated; then Blyth uttered a harsh whinny and the horse raced off into the trees. Blyth hoped that it would be alright and might find a herd to join.

"Istum ligate!" ordered Lucius.

Blyth was tied tightly by hands and feet and slung over the pack mule, and the contubernium prepared to move on.

Back at the grove a teacher and two students, who had gone in search of Blyth, arrived back at dusk with no news. Teague and Abbon were worried and accused the teacher of not trying hard enough.

"You don't care what happens to him do you?" said Teague, fighting back tears.

"Gwenn will find him," he said, "don't worry."

'Don't worry?' What does he know?' thought Teague. But Teague was not someone who voiced everything he thought, as Blyth was. Teague let it simmer while he decided what to do. He pulled Abbon away to the hut and told him that they would leave before dawn the next day and go in search of their brother themselves. Abbon was scared but determined.

They may have had their fights over the years but in times of trouble they stuck together.

That same day, long before dawn, Teague was awake and packing silently. His keen eyes were able to see in the dark better than anyone he knew and his methodical mind missing nothing that might be needed. He had lain awake most of the night thinking and planning what they would do. The search party had said they followed Gwenn's trail south down the river so that was the way he and Abbon would go. He woke Abbon, and the two boys crept out of the hut and untied their horses. Snow lay thickly on the ground and the only sound as they rode out of the camp was the crunch-crunch of horses' hooves on the thick carpet of white. By the time the sun was properly up they were already far away from camp and hot on the heels of their brother. As the sun set they had reached the place where Blyth had been at sunrise the day before. Teague urged Abbon to continue and they rode on into the depths of night, aided by copious quantities of strong morning tea which Teague prepared whenever they stopped. Their bodies were wired awake as they rode steadfastly on through the night at a good solid pace, but by midnight the horses could take no more and Teague admitted they would have to stop. A few hours later, as dawn broke once more, they mounted up and continued on their way. They had been riding for a few hours and the sun was nearly at its highest point when they spotted Gwenn ahead of them. She was talking to a stranger who was pointing and appeared to be giving directions. They rode on to meet her as she parted company with the stranger.

"Hi, any news?" called Teague, as if he and Abbon being here was all part of the plan.

"Why aren't you back at the grove?" she asked pointedly.

"And leave our brother to die in the snow?"

"He's not in the snow is he?"

They were just a few thousand paces from the southern sea and, whilst it was far from warm, the sun was shining and it could not in any way be described as snowy.

"Well we didn't know that. Besides where is he? Have you found him?

"He has been taken by Romani warriors. They're heading to Narbo, the capital of this region."

"Well come on, what are we waiting for?" said Teague.

"Yeah come on, let's get 'em," echoed Abbon.

"Have either of you eaten?" Gwenn enquired. She looked at their thin faces, as white as sheets, and saw their eyes, glazed and rimmed with dark circles. "Or slept?" she added.

"Well..." said Abbon.

"We'll worry about that when we find Blyth," insisted Teague.

"And will you be in any fit state to help him, if and when you do find him?"

"Erm…" Teague was stuck for an answer.

Gwenn led the horses to the river and helped the boys dismount. She pointed her staff at the ground and a blazing fire erupted from the end and crackled merrily as if it had been alight all morning. She pulled some food from her pack and tossed strips of boar meat and chunks of thick bread to the boys. They drank from the river and Gwenn filled them in on the situation. After nearly thirty hours awake, under the influence of Teague's tea, Abbon soon drifted into a deep sleep. Teague dozed off shortly afterwards despite manfully trying to fight it.

Gwenn loaded the two across their horses like saddle packs and slowly led them along the path in the direction the stranger had indicated. At nightfall she found an overhanging rock and made the best of the natural shelter. Further enquiries from friendly locals had established that they were not far behind the soldiers who had taken Blyth. She knew the patrol would camp for the night, and that she could catch up easily on horseback, while the soldiers were on foot. What she did not want to do was to catch up while they were still at a disadvantage. At dawn she woke up to find Teague already brewing tea.

"Ready to rescue your brother now?" she said, her head on one side.

"If he hasn't already been killed. You slowed us down."

She ignored the comment. "Is there enough tea for

me?"

"I suppose so."

Teague couldn't stay angry with anyone for long. Whereas Blyth boiled over at the slightest provocation and took ages to calm down, Teague almost never lost his temper and when he did, it was short, sharp, and then over. They woke Abbon and drank the tea silently, ate some of the bread and the last of the boar and then mounted up and rode after the contubernium.

They caught up with the Romans before mid-day, hanging back just close enough to observe but not be noticed. Blyth was walking now, tied between two soldiers, and struggling futilely every now and then. The Decanus hit him with a stick but he threw himself on the floor and had to be dragged along. Lucius was beginning to think he would be better off letting him go for all the trouble he was causing but somehow he suspected that Blyth might be more than he seemed.

Gwenn told Teague and Abbon to ride in a big arc to get ahead of the patrol and to keep out of sight until they received her signal.

With her staff she created a disturbance in the trees which distracted the patrol. Lucius sent two of his men into the undergrowth to see who was there. Another spell caused a small rock-slide on the other side of the road as if someone was moving there. The patrol was on edge and looking in every direction. Lucius sent another two men to investigate among the rocks leaving just himself, three other soldiers and the two servants, around Blyth. Gwenn now rode the stallion straight towards the men and dismounted. She threw something towards them which burst into smoke as it struck the ground. The Decanus led his remaining men in a chase after the tall druid who dared to attack them. She left her horse and turned and ran, leading them away from Blyth, while the stallion waited. Then the horse trotted to where Blyth stood. Blyth just about managed to clamber onto its back but then watched with terror as the soldiers closed on Gwenn. Just as it seemed inevitable that she would be caught he watched astounded as she leapt and transformed in mid-flight into a snow white mare. The soldiers stumbled and fell over each other as she accelerated away, turning only to see that Blyth was safe. He could not ride properly as he was still tied up but she cantered to his side and guided the stallion to meet up with Teague and Abbon.

"Blyth!" they called in unison, as he rode up on Gwenn's horse with the matching white mare beside them.

"What happened to Gwenn?" Teague asked.

"Umm…" Blyth hesitated.

The white mare transformed again, into the tall pale haired beauty that was Gwenn; the boys simply stared open mouthed.

"No time for questions," she said. "We need to get out of here, out of Romani territory, before they send a whole legion to catch us. I broke the most basic rule by letting them see me transform. I just hope nobody believes their story."

They untied Blyth and started making their way north and east as fast as they could. Blyth regretted the loss of his fiery wild-eyed stallion. But they had formed a strong bond, stronger than Blyth realized. The next day the roan stallion reappeared as they reached the split in the river where Blyth had collapsed the day before. Blyth was overjoyed and lavished praise and grooming on his much-loved steed. The four followed the river north, upstream, to the safety of Keltoi territory.

14

They could not return to the grove; Gwenn had received word that the three boys would not be welcome back. Up to now they had learned to recite the stories of creation and of the Gods, as well as other legends. They had learned much about nature and the uses of plants for medicine, as well as what Kaito had taught them. The next year would have involved learning magic. Not all the students could learn magic; it was something you were either born to or not. Some went on to study music and poetry and became bards. Some would specialize in medicine and go back to their clans as healers. Others would go on to become administrators, or carry out ceremonies and rituals. But the most powerful Deru-Weidi were those who learned magic and became advisers to powerful tribal leaders and Kings. The King would wield power in name only; the real power behind the throne was the mage who advised him.

Now it fell to Gwenn to continue their education. She had sworn an oath to Trethiwr, when she had last seen him. He was travelling home from his long travels and he told her that he was going to die. He asked her to swear, by the Sky and the Sea and the Earth, to prepare his sons for a quest that they would have to undertake and she had sworn there and then.

Now she decided to avoid contact with the Deru-Weidi completely, and to teach them her own special magic. She led them east, following the river, to a huge lake. It was slate blue under heavy leaden skies; white rimes of ice clogged up the edges and coated fallen branches and clumps of reeds. They carried on along the north side of the lake, the southern shore marking the extent of Roman territory. To the east, huge ice-covered mountains rose up before them. They camped on the northern shore and the next day they turned north and continued to another lake, which they then followed along the southern shore. The terrain was very steep and rocky, and everywhere there were lakes and rivers large and small; the smaller ones were frozen over completely. The weather tended to be cold but dry, the sun felt hot when it shone directly on them but any cloud cover made it seem chilly and the breeze doubled the effect when it blew. They passed farms and small villages and several of the locals hailed Gwenn as she passed, some even coming to chat in a thick dialect which the boys could not follow.

"How come so many people know you?" asked Teague, who noticed things like that.

"We will be in my home village by nightfall," she told him, smiling with pleasure at the thought of seeing some of her family.

After a few hours' riding they saw another, smaller, lake to the right and they rode along a snow-covered ridge, a mere couple of thousand paces to either lake shore. The road turned north, passing around the end of the larger lake on their left, and they headed for a large, low hill which Gwenn told them was her home. The village of Entwalen-Dun, hill between two lakes, was at least twice the size of Maywr-Dun and enjoyed the most spectacular views along two long valleys, with the sun reflecting on the cold slate blue waters of the lakes. To the south-east, foothills stumbled into mountains, crumpling the ground into heaps of jumbled stone, giving way to more and more contortions of rock, piled high with turrets and towers and dusted with increasing amounts of ice and snow. Teetering blocks defied gravity, building with distance into a series of jagged white teeth as if the whole Earth was a vast dragon and this was its mouth.

The boys soon picked up the strange accent spoken by Gwenn's friends and family. Most of the words were the same, or similar, but the way they pronounced them differed quite markedly, but once it clicked it became easy.

They met Gwenn's brothers and sisters, and her

nieces and nephews. The Mage was an old friend of her parents who had spotted her magical potential.

After the introductions had evidently finished, Teague asked Gwenn if she had any children. Others might have avoided the subject as there had been no mention of the subject but Teague was always quite direct and matter-of-fact about things.

"I cannot have children," she told him in a similarly matter-of-fact way.

Teague was not the sort of person who might consider leaving it at that. He was not inconsiderate but he simply didn't know a touchy subject when he saw one.

"Why?"

"Maybe I'll tell you one day," she said. "Now don't ask any more questions. You have a hard day ahead of you. No doubt you will find many more difficult questions to ask then."

The next day was typically cold, and dry. Faint wisps of cloud blew over, stopping Bellenos from warming them as he should. Gwenn took them out walking; she made a point of making sure the horses were left behind, beside the northern lake which disappeared in a point at the valley head. She led them to a wide rushing stream which ran down from the hills. The water was icy cold and swift. It was about ten full paces from bank to bank and there was no sign of a bridge or a ford.

"Let's cross here," she said.

"Erm, I don't think so!" insisted Blyth. "Not unless

we want to get swept away and frozen to death."

"There are a hundred Romani soldiers coming up the path behind us and this is the only way to escape them," she said.

"No there aren't!" stated Blyth simply. "And anyway, we could just follow it upstream until there was a crossing point."

"I know there aren't really a hundred soldiers following us, but if there were how could we cross without horses?"

"Head upstream," reiterated Blyth.

"There isn't time; they are right behind you."

"I reckon I could climb," piped up Abbon. "There's plenty of tree cover," he added.

"OK, let's say you are safely across. Will you leave Teague and Abbon?"

"No; not after all we've been through."

"Any other suggestions?"

"We could cut down a tree and make it fall across."

"They are right behind you remember? Besides, then they just follow you across the same tree."

"Rope!" said Blyth.

"Go on?"

He indicated a branch which reached out over the stream.

"Erm, throw a rope over that branch, and swing over. Then pull it back when we are all across."

"Might work, if you had a rope on you. How about this?" she said.

Then she amazed them once again by transforming into the snow white mare that she had become during her daring rescue of Blyth. With considerable ease she made the leap across the stream and then at a canter she turned and jumped back across, transforming back into Gwenn moments after she landed.

"Yeah... right... well it might have escaped your attention but we can't all turn into horses can we?" Blyth said. He was beginning to master the art of sarcasm. "Or were you planning on carrying us over one by one? You did mention a couple of times that they were supposedly right behind us!"

"Your task is to learn to do what I have just shown you," said Gwenn, annoyed by Blyth's negativity.

Abbon was excited. "We're going to turn into horses! Great!" he added.

"Not necessarily horses. You choose your animal. Some choose birds; a raven is popular, or an owl. Some wizards can turn into many different forms. You have to start with something you feel comfortable with, something you have an affinity for or that perhaps shares your characteristics."

Abbon thought back to a sunny day in the grove some months ago, and it came to him.

"A squirrel!" he announced. "If I could turn into a squirrel I could climb the trees even faster. I could escape, or I could just as easily hide." Abbon had never been so excited.

Blyth on the other hand was dejected and hopeless.

"I don't have any affinity with animals. I'm not even any good as a hunter." A particular hunt stood out in his memory when he had missed twice, and then had to have the prey practically imprisoned before he could manage to kill anything.

"Come on Blyth, you can do it," Teague encouraged him. "Your name is wolf after all why not try and be a wolf?"

Blyth crossed his arms and turned his back on them.

Gwenn sighed: it was going to be a long summer.

"You don't have to decide yet, any of you. Let's head back to the village; we can eat and sleep and you can let me know your thoughts tomorrow."

It took months of work before they were even ready to start learning about the complex magic involved in learning to transform into an animal. First they had to decide on which animal to become. Abbon stuck with his first choice, a squirrel. Teague toyed with a horse, and a raven, as well as asking about fish, which Gwen strongly discouraged, before finally deciding that some sort of wild cat would be suitably deadly whilst maintaining an air of mystery and intelligence. Blyth couldn't think of anything, but grudgingly agreed to consider the wolf idea.

The next step was to learn as much about their chosen creature as possible. Abbon spent hours watching squirrels in the trees around the village, finding their hollowed out nests in the trunks, watching as they carefully held on to small pieces of food with tiny little clawed fingers, nibbling briefly before looking in all directions for any sign of danger, then continuing with another tiny morsel and checking again. They were always moving, always on edge, and always alert. The big bushy tail flicked, this way and that, as they scampered up the trunks of trees with the merest suggestion of something to hold on to, and scurried along the thinnest branches leaping from the end and clearing, sometimes, ten or twelve paces of clear air before landing on the further branch tip and scrambling along it to the next tree.

Teague sat up half the night trying to watch his chosen animals but only saw the briefest glimpse of one in the distance. Gwenn however, somehow managed to obtain a pair of kittens. She didn't say where they came from. They were small, about a hand span from nose to the base of the tail, but they were tough with very sharp teeth and claws. Gwenn had a large enclosure built for them with enough space for them to run and play. This meant that Teague could watch them any time he wanted, which was practically all the time. He found it particularly gratifying that they slept for large portions of the day and were most active before dawn and after sunset. Gwenn gave up trying to get him to come for meals and just delivered strips of meat and bread to Teague who told her new things he had discovered every time he saw her.

Blyth got off to a slow start being wholly disinterested in the entire exercise. Gwenn avoided putting too much pressure on him, preferring to allow him to decide in his own time. Blyth was giving serious thought to running away but couldn't decide where to. As long as Gwenn was keeping off his back he decided to stick around. He spent some time mooching about the village, watching the craftsmen at work. Otherwise he would wander through the woods, kicking leaves, or along the lake shores, idly skimming stones.

Gwenn watched him from a distance, biding her time and wondering what his father had foreseen.

15

Winter gave way to spring grudgingly here, nestled between high mountains. There were occasional snow showers throughout the next three months right up to the festival of Belotenios, marking the beginning of the second half of the year, summer. In Entwalen-Dun the celebrations were huge; perhaps the need for change was greater here than in most places. Snow lay thick on all but the lowest slopes as Bellenos began the arduous task of melting it.

There were large animal enclosures in the village, where most of the livestock could be kept during the worst of the winter. The cattle were already there and the sheep and goats were brought in from the fields to join them. Firewood was collected in two huge pyres towering twice the height of Gwenn and spaced about fifty paces apart. They were lit a little before sunset and, as the great immortal fire of Bellenos melted into the western waters, the two mortal fires blazed high into the sky sending sparks dancing into the deepening blue.

The heat could be felt thirty paces away, and became too intense to bear within fifteen, yet the whole herd, not just a few token animals, was driven headlong between them with a cacophony of terrified bleating and lowing. This would purify the animals both physically and spiritually, ensuring good milk yields and fertility. The feast was the most stupendous the boys had ever seen. Tables groaned under the weight of whole wild boar, roasted sheep, sides of oxen, and chickens; the fat glistening in the light of the two huge fires, now slowly dying down, and the flickering of hundreds of torches mounted on tall poles. Once the Chief, the warriors, and the elders of the village had taken the choicest cuts and the Deru-Weido had taken a share for the Gods, the rest of the village, including the boys and Gwenn, took their share and went to sit down. Gwenn avoided the meat and instead loaded her dish up with a wide selection of vegetables and wild mushrooms as well as slabs of heavy, seedy bread and freshly made butter.

Whilst the warriors and farmers, men and women alike, all drank prodigious quantities of wine or beer, Gwenn kept to an infusion of herbs. As night drew in, villagers began to head back to their huts and the torchlight died down. As was often the case many, including Teague and Abbon, slept where they had sat. It was a clear, cold night but the fires would still give off a lot of heat right through until dawn. Blyth was still wide awake when Gwenn suggested they go for a walk before going to their huts.

Blyth agreed and, pulling his cloak round him, he got up. They strolled off towards the north-eastern end of the village, where they could look out along the great finger of water that stretched away between the mountains on either side. The full moon shone like a silver coin on the black surface of the lake, which was as smooth as glass. Leaning on her staff Gwenn looked straight at Blyth and asked, "How do you feel about your father?"

Blyth looked uncomfortable. He wasn't at all sure how he felt. His father had hardly ever been there while he was growing up, and then he had gone and got himself killed just when he seemed to be back for good. Blyth felt cheated, and worse he felt like he was being manipulated. He just wanted an easy life: his horse, his brothers, good hunting, warm fires, a village where he belonged, his mother and Elarch. An image of Blodwyth dressed in flowing white robes flitted across his mind. He shook his head to clear it and spoke slowly.

"I think that he deserted us, and what I really miss is waking up in my hut with my family, and knowing where I am."

"He did desert you, in a sense, but he foresaw something and you were a big part of it. He said that your future was tied in with a boy, born on the same day, who was associated with wolves. That is why he called you Blyth."

"I've heard something about this. But I don't want to go on any quest or fight any battles. I just want… " he hesitated as the image of Blodwyth flitted across his mind again.

"I'm sorry Blyth; I believe the Gods have chosen your path."

"What if I choose to ignore it?"

"I think you know that you can't."

Blyth turned his back on her.

"I'm going to try!"

Gwenn sighed. "Come on, let's get back. It's too cold to defy the Gods tonight. You can make a start in the morning."

Blyth missed her subtle joke. That night he slept fitfully and Blodwyth featured heavily in his dreams.

He saw her dressed in her flowing white Imbolc robes in a dark forest. There were dozens of stags fighting amongst themselves. The great antlers crashed into each other, time and time again, shaking the very ground and the trees above them, and yet she stood amongst these fearsome creatures unmoved. Then suddenly they were surrounded by a pack of wolves; some of the stags turned their attention to fending off the wolves but many continued to fight each other, ignoring the threat, and a few actually joined with the wolf pack and attacked those which were doing the defending. Blodwyth held up branches of burning oak to try and hold them off but slowly the wolves devoured almost all of the stags. Blodwyth mounted one of the last stags and a handful of them escaped across a broad stream and, as the light of her torches flickered, he saw the wolves closing in with the darkness, and then he woke up sweating and shivering at the same time. He lay awake, wondering what this meant for some time, before finally drifting off again.

Teague was up before dawn, poking the embers for a bit of warmth. There were plenty of leftovers around and he warmed a piece of bread over the awakened fire and watched the first glint of bright sunlight edge over the horizon. He set about brewing up some morning tea and woke Abbon with a cup. Then they went off in search of Blyth. They found him curled up in several furs but no amount of prodding would wake him, so they left him and looked for Gwenn instead. Gwenn didn't appear surprised that he was not with them.

"He was up very late last night, leave him. We don't have to do anything today and he will be the better for a good night's sleep."

The two younger boys went off to play in the woods but Gwenn kept close to Blyth's hut ready for when he should wake up. It was almost mid-day when he finally emerged, blinking in the bright light. Gwenn was loitering close to the smith's forge which was in line of sight of the boy's hut. He scowled at the unkind sun, and half closed his eyes against its brightness; pulling his cloak around him he shuffled over to where Gwenn stood and watched the sparks flying as the smith mercilessly pounded a strip of iron into a horseshoe. It was warm here; the forge gave off a fierce heat. The smith's brow glistened with sweat and glowed like the roast boar at the feast.

"Did you sleep well?" enquired Gwenn.

"Not really, I had a bad dream."

Gwenn said nothing, but watched him patiently. Blyth filled in the silence reluctantly but automatically.

"There was a girl from my old village. She was 'Brigantia' at my last Imbolc feast there."

Gwenn remained silent and attentive, leaving an empty void of silence which Blyth could not help but fill. He explained all about his dream and asked, "What does it all mean?"

"I think she represents our way of life," replied Gwenn.

"So she's not in danger?"

"Not now, but the wolves could represent the Romani. They are organized, like a wolf pack, with a leader and a strong hierarchy. Our people are divided into many different tribes and we fight amongst ourselves like stags in the woods. Is the girl important to you?" she asked him.

Blyth did not answer but turned and walked a little way away. He wasn't sure what he felt about Blodwyth, and he didn't feel like trying to explain it to anyone else right now.

"Maybe this is part of what your father could see," called Gwenn, changing the subject. "He predicted that the Romani would continue to take over Keltoi lands until there was nothing left. He also said they would stop at nothing to stamp out our use of magic and our Gods. It is already happening in the south. Trethiwr believed that it was only a matter of time before they try to take over here as well, and then on to your own island. Perhaps that was the part about the stream?"

"So what can I do?" said Blyth grumpily.

"I don't know, but I'm certain that you cannot escape your destiny."

16

Summer came to Entwalen-Dun; there were long days of warm sunshine and the low slopes turned an incredible vivid green, although it never got oppressively hot, and the highest mountains retained a perpetual cloak of white. Every few days the atmosphere would become loaded and heavy, and this was followed invariably by a tumultuous thunderstorm. At night it lit up the sky: Leucretios, with every relentless lash, momentarily rending the black satin veil of night and revealing a flash of the light beyond, Taranis following up each flash of light with a tremendous crash of thunder. During the day, the rain fell so hard that it could soak you to the skin in the time it took to run from one hut to another. Farmers out in the fields simply carried on working and when the rain stopped and the sun made its apologetic appearance they steamed quietly as they dried out.

Soon there was the festival of Lughunasath and

more bonfires and feasting. Just two days after the feast there was a raid on some of the cattle, on a farm to the north of the village. The farmer was killed but his son escaped and rode to the village on a pony to seek help from the Chief. A band of warriors quickly rode out to chase the bandits, following directions given by the young lad. Gwenn went with them; transformed into a horse she had a considerable weight advantage over the mounted warriors and she went on ahead. There were about twenty armed and mounted warriors driving thirty head of cattle ahead of them north east along the north side of the lake. She passed them with ease, eliciting curious and avaricious stares from the surprised bandits, as she galloped out of sight past a bend in the pass. The way became narrow here, bounded by the lake on the right and steep slopes on the left. She returned to her human form and, using some powerful magic, she caused a rock slide which blocked the path. Then, exhausted, she climbed up to a higher ledge and took cover in some bushes.

The cattle were milling about, while the bandits tried to find a way through. There was a track which turned back on the path and wound up between the rocks, but it was too steep for the cattle. Soon the warriors from the village caught up with them, and in the ensuing skirmish one of the warriors from the village was mortally wounded when a spear penetrated his chest. He was lying clutching the shaft of the spear and coughing up pink frothy blood when Gwenn reached him and there was clearly nothing she could do, although she invoked Lenus, a God of healing, in a vain attempt to save him. His killer and another man were slain at the same time but the rest of the bandits fled, chased by most of the remaining warriors determined for revenge. Three remained with Gwenn who pulled the spear from the warrior's lifeless body, and closed his wild staring eyes. They rounded up the small herd and loaded their fallen comrade across his horse before heading back to Entwalen-Dun.

The dead man, Durgal, was a nephew of the Chief and had fought well and loyally for many years, defending the local peasants as well as leading the war band in a major battle with a neighbouring tribe some years earlier. His funeral would be a major event and messengers were sent out to kinfolk and friendly local Chiefs to attend. His body was adorned with the finest the village had to offer, the best armour, including a breastplate which belonged to the Chief, and a sword made specially for him by the smith. The hilt was made of bronze, shaped to represent a man, the head a detailed representation of Durgal, down to the crooked nose and the scar on his cheek gained in his first battle. He was dressed in the finest clothes, woven from linen and wool, dyed in bright colours and fastened with brooches of bronze and silver, and he wore neck and arm torcs wound from several thick strands of gold.

The heads of the dead bandits were mounted on spears and carried alongside the bier, which was lifted onto a funeral pyre, eight feet high, which had been built outside the walls to the west. The fire was lit and began to burn until the heat was too intense to bear within ten paces. It burned well into the night and the mourners returned to Entwalen-Dun for feasting, and for stories focusing on the brave deeds of Durgal. The next day the remains were buried close to the lake and the guests made sacrifices to the Gods for their departed friend. This involved making long speeches and casting treasured possessions, including swords, shields, torcs, and spears, into the lake. There was even a chariot which was wheeled to the end of a jetty and hurled bodily into the black and icy waters by four burly warriors.

Apart from this there was little to distract the boys from their studies and, by the end of summer, Teague and Abbon had learned enough about their chosen animals to satisfy Gwenn. When Blyth was off wandering somewhere, she took the other two aside and told them what they would need to do next. At a carefully conducted ceremony they would have to kill one of their chosen animals and eat certain parts of it. This was to allow the spirit of the animal into themselves and to make the transformation possible. Of course, they had both seen enough animal sacrifices to accept the idea in principle but Teague was upset, having spent more than eight months with the pair of kittens. He had watched them grow from small but deadly cuddly toys into sleek young adults, and he had grown emotionally attached to them. Abbon was not in the least bit worried about killing a squirrel; he had killed enough while practicing with his trusty sling. Gwenn reassured Teague that they would need a wild cat which had not been contaminated by contact with humans and they set about hunting for a suitable victim. Blyth was excluded from all this activity as he had not completed any of the preliminaries and could not be party to the next step.

Teague and Abbon, sworn to secrecy, went with Gwenn and once again experienced the magical hunting technique used by their father on their one and only hunting trip with him. They began at sunset and nothing happened for a long time. It was very dark, with clouds hiding the almost full moon for most of the time. It wasn't particularly cold but Teague shivered as they watched the invisible circle drawn by Gwenn.

"It's not working is it?" he wondered out loud.

"It takes time," Gwenn whispered, "shhh."

Teague dropped his voice to a barely audible whisper, "When father did this, before he... well anyway it took only a few minutes."

"I set it up for cats only," Gwen whispered back. "It might take all night, or not work at all. It won't if we don't keep quiet."

Teague took the hint and said nothing more. He drew his cloak about him and sat hunched up staring intently at the spot where they hoped a wild cat would stroll in and patiently await its fate. Abbon dozed off shortly afterwards and Teague was fast asleep within the hour. Gwenn sat in stony silence sipping from a skin bottle to keep herself awake.

By dawn there was still no sign of a cat and Gwenn woke the boys and headed back to the village. The next night was the same and Teague told Gwenn that he thought he could sacrifice one of his cats if he had to. Again she assured him that the cats were not ideal, because they were domesticated, and she would prefer to catch a wild one, so they went out for a third night. It was towards the end of the night, as the sky was just beginning to turn from black to indigo and the two boys slumbered quietly, that a male cat with pronounced dark stripes slinked into the circle and prowled around a few times before laying down as if to sleep. Gwenn had been awake for three nights and days without a break and even with the special tea she was drinking, she was beginning to doze off herself. It took a few minutes before she realized that she wasn't dreaming of a cat, and was actually looking at the real thing. She nudged Teague, who stirred and opened his eyes. Seeing the cat sparked him into wakefulness and he got up quickly. He had no idea what to do next; all his thoughts had been about getting a cat in the first place and now he flapped and flustered as Gwenn tried to calm him down. She had thought ahead however, and produced a sack which she gave to Teague and told him to capture the cat alive, which he did without much trouble. They woke Abbon and told him the good news and then Gwenn set up a trap for a squirrel. This did not take long and they had a choice of specimens by lunchtime.

The real business would take place at the next new moon, meanwhile the two animals were caged in a hut and the boys were forbidden to enter. Gwenn fed the animals for the next week until the new moon, and they prepared for the sacrifice. Under the total darkness of a cloudy moonless sky Gwenn led the two boys and their sacrificial animals to a clearing surrounded by ancient oak trees. The squirrel squirmed and wriggled ineffectually in Abbon's firm yet gentle grip and its body went slack as he drew a deadly sharp iron blade across its throat. The cat gave Teague rather more trouble scratching him several times with it razor sharp claws and trying to sink its teeth into his wrist as he drew the blade across its pale beige neck, but eventually it too lay limp and bloodied.

Gwenn butchered the carcasses and removed the liver, heart and brains. These she cut up and gave small pieces of each to the boys. Gwenn drew a circle with her staff and instructed the boys to eat the meat while she recited ancient words. Then she made the boys recite an oath.

"I swear that I will use my powers to protect my family and my tribe before all others. I swear that I will use my powers for good and not for evil. I swear that I will not teach these powers to anyone not of my tribe. I swear that I will not teach these powers to anyone not worthy to wield them. If I should break this oath then may the sky fall down upon my head, may the seas rise up and drown me, may the earth open up and swallow me."

"Nothing's happened," said Teague.

"Now you have to consciously think of transforming. It requires concentration. Focus on your animal now."

Abbon and Teague did so. Teague transformed first, becoming the image of the cat that he had just sacrificed, a pale yellowy beige on the belly, darkening to a rich amber on the back with strong dark stripes. Sleek and powerful, he turned and paced around stretching his legs and testing his new muscles and bones. Abbon transformed a few moments later and quickly scampered up a tree and along a branch to the thinnest point that could support his weight, where he immediately slipped and fell off, landing with a fluffy thud on the back of his feline brother. Teague leapt at Abbon who skittered away and returned to his normal shape in a bundle of dirt and leaf litter. Teague landed on him and almost sank claws in as he too changed back to human form on top of his brother.

"Get off me! What do you think you were doing?"

"Sorry I couldn't help it; I just felt an overwhelming urge to attack you."

"Well don't."

"How come you fell off anyway?"

Gwenn interrupted, "You will both take a little time to get used to your new bodies and learn to judge your abilities. Abbon will take some time to get used to what he can or can't do up a tree and you, Teague, will need to learn to control your cat instincts while you are transformed. You must not stay transformed for too long or you may forget that you are human and never turn back."

Teague nodded, and both boys transformed again. This time they played among the trees as they made their way back to the village following Gwenn, who chose to remain human, maintaining a little dignity as the cat and the squirrel rolled around on the floor or chased up and down trees.

17

The next day Blyth was as surly and obstinate as ever and Gwenn decided that they needed a change of scenery.

"Let's go on a journey," she suggested over breakfast. Teague and Abbon had transformed repeatedly already that morning, much to Blyth's annoyance; but rather than making him more determined to learn the transformation himself, he simply shut out the idea. He wasn't going to be some childish idiot, like his brothers, changing shape all the time just for a laugh. He respected Gwenn of course but he wasn't going to admit that, as she might start trying to persuade him again. Instead he grudgingly agreed to her suggestion of a journey and left it at that.

Gwenn insisted on waiting until the new moon to commence any long journey, for good luck. She also wanted to make a sacrifice to Lugh, whose many duties included taking care of travellers. So on the day of the new moon they climbed to the highest point of the ridge, to the north of the village, that loomed over the great lake, with one of the lambs from that spring, and waited for sunset. The mountain was white with snow and ice, and the sky was a fierce blue with a few thin wisps of cloud to the West. Even as the sun began to set, turning the tips of the snowy mountains pink and turning the surface of the lake to fiery orange, a dark patch appeared across the edge of the setting sun. They did not notice, at first, as they were preparing the lamb for the sacrifice, but as they turned to look at the disappearing disc of Bellenos, racing towards the night, there was already a large bite taken out of the edge and it was getting larger all the time. Their eyes hurt to look at it and yet they were drawn inexorably to glance, as long as they could bear it, at the horrifying sight of Bellenos, the sun God, being consumed by the dark moon. As they stared through half closed lids the sun sank below the horizon not fully obscured but yet seemingly losing the battle against the ravenous moon. Quickly Gwenn remembered the lamb and made a sacrifice for the safe passage of Bellenos through the night to the next day and they set off back to the village.

In the village there was a great deal of activity. Everyone had witnessed the apparent battle between light and dark. Coming so soon after Samonios, the New Year, with the village in the grip of winter, and the longest night less than a fortnight away, the people were terrified. Babies cried, men and women uttered prayers and recited poems to ward off evil, the animals were spooked and there was a hubbub of lowing and bleating and squawking filling the air. The Deru-Weido Mage was directing activity; it was clear to all that a tremendous battle was taking place between the forces of darkness and chaos led by Dis-Fater against the forces of light lead by Lugh, bonfires were being built and sacrifices made, and people were crying, and gathering their families around them. One woman leapt into the flames of one of the larger pyres and screamed, with her dying breath, for Lugh to welcome her into his halls. Amid this scene of chaos, Gwenn calmly led the boys to their house and made them drink a sleep tea, before sitting up by the fire watching the flames flickering over the wood and the first flakes of snow falling from the deep grey sky. She left the village and headed for the forests to the south west. Using her magic she was able to attract a small bird with a patch of bright gold on its head. She held the bird gently in her hand and carried it back to the village.

The next morning, the first of the month of Riurios, 'moon of darkest nights', was freezing cold, with the snow lying thick on the ground. It was well before sunrise as Gwenn stood alone looking out at the mountain range to the south east, awaiting the rising sun. Her breath formed wreaths of smoke, echoing the smouldering fires of the previous evening. The villagers had realised that death and destruction had not come to them yet; they were tired and cold, and now they were asleep in their houses dreaming fitfully.

It was a cloudless night, the snows had come and gone, the stars were stunningly bright, each group clear in the sky. Dis-Fater stood, with his belt and club, surveying his dark domain. Cernunnos with his horns; the horse goddess, Epona, prancing across the black veil of night, and there was Lugh's chariot pointing the way to the north.

Using the stars as a guide, she calculated the point at which the sun would rise, and she watched and waited patiently to make the appropriate sacrifice. Even she was not certain what the day would bring but, as the dawn approached, the sky began to lighten by imperceptible degrees and the first hint of birdsong began, just as the first golden rays blazed proudly over the jagged peaks to the South East. Gwenn smiled a wan smile of relief as she raised the blade, cut swiftly through the neck of the small bird in her hand, and uttered a prayer of thanks to Lugh.

Bellenos rose proudly above the dark teeth of the mountain range, clearly none the worse for his night's battle. Despite this, Gwenn decided to put off their journey for a while. Winter, she reasoned, was no time to travel. She was needed here to show the people that there was nothing to fear. And so it was three moons later, immediately after Imbolc, that the four of them set out on their delayed journey.

The first part of the trip was uneventful. They

retraced the route taken by Blyth when he ran away from the Deru-Weidi at the end of the previous winter, but taking the pace quite a bit more slowly this time. They travelled as traders heading for the ancient port of Massalia, on the coast to the south, and swapping stories on the way. Gwenn traded her skills at small villages in exchange for commodities that would sell in Rome. At one village they met a Dwr-Y-Tryges trader who was a distant cousin of the boys and he updated them on the news of their old home, although little of it was good. Food had become scarce and there was constant fighting over limited resources; many of their friends had been killed although the tribe was usually victorious. The trader was ill, so Gwenn gave him medicine and used magic to make him well, and in exchange he insisted that they take a dozen hunting dogs that he had been going to trade in Massalia. By the time they arrived in Massalia they had a convincing cargo of hides and furs, silver, tin, and gems, loaded onto a cart, with the dozen dogs tied to the back.

The ancient Hellenic port was the busiest place the boys had ever seen, teeming with life and colour. Every sense was assaulted at once. People from every part of the world jostled in the marketplace: Helleni; Romani; Keltoi and dark skinned people, of unfamiliar tribes; traders, from every part of the southern sea - the 'Mare Nostrum' as the Romani called it. Myriad colours, vibrant in the brilliant sun: burning reds and yellows, eye-aching whites, the glint of iron on a spear, the earthy brown of leather, the sheen of polished bronze, glittering jewellery, deep sky-blue robes of wealthy merchants, and the purple-striped aristocracy filled their vision.

Their noses were filled with the smell of goats and cattle, chickens and geese, the fresh smell of grass, the delicious aroma of a thousand spices and fresh herbs, locally grown olive oil, and the pungent smell of honest sweat. Wine waited in ranks of large clay pots to be traded, perhaps to a Ligurian merchant in exchange for slaves. The noise was a continual babble of conversation on every subject from politics to the weather, stabbed intermittently by the loud calls of traders offering their wares for sale. Food vendors enticed the small group to come and taste their home cooking. On offer were flat breads, soaked with oil and herbs and topped with vegetables, thick rich barley soups, strong-smelling cheeses and strips of smoked and dried meat, as well as wine and beer to drink. Gwenn rebuffed their eager advances, even lifting one small but noisy man bodily out of her way. She led the boys to a quieter part of the town where there was a small inn - simple, clean, and filled with local people.

They saw to the horses and dogs and made sure the cart with their cargo was safe before finding a table in the inn. They sat in a corner next to a group who were talking loudly and animatedly in Latin. Gwenn ordered in the local dialect, which owed as much to the Helleni as it did to Liguria. Massalia had been a Hellenic port since before anyone could remember, before Brynno had sacked Rome in fact, and their influence spread widely across the region. Helleni and Galli had long been loose allies, joining forces against the Romani on many occasions, and there were even Gallic tribes living far to the east by the eastern sea, although, now, it was Roman influence here that kept Massalia as an independent port.

After their meal Gwenn told the boys to stay with the horses. She continued on down to the docks to engage passage on a merchant vessel. Trading on the Mare Nostrum was relatively safe. The Romani fleet kept piracy to a minimum. Trade was the lifeblood of Rome and their complete supremacy in the region brought with it great political and military stability. Gwenn found a Gallic trading vessel, feeling they would blend in better with their own people. It was around twenty paces long with a single mast, a lower storage deck, and a wide flat bottom. There was room for the four travellers and their various goods. She agreed a price with the captain and paid half in advance as security, and then she returned to the inn.

Early the next morning the boys and Gwenn loaded the wagon onto the ship. It was already carrying a large cargo of wheat grain which had been loaded over the previous two days. Several seasoned traders mingled on deck with a variety of merchandise. Gwenn and the boys attracted many whispers and suspicious glances. They were new faces in a well-established business and their cargo was valuable including, as it did, a large amount of precious tin. Blyth however, who was in a particularly good mood that morning, chatted freely with some of the traders and his Pretanic dialect soothed some of their suspicions. Of course a young man from Pretan on his first trading voyage might be expected to have tin, and hunting dogs. It made sense. Gwenn uneased people at the best of times, she was the most striking woman they were ever likely to see, with her long platinum blonde hair, her tall muscular frame, fine facial features and piercing blue eyes. Eventually it was agreed that she must have been hired to keep the young merchant and his brothers safe. Once again the journey passed without major incident and after three days hugging the coastline the trading ship approached the port of Ostia, the lifeblood of the greatest city in the known world.

Impressed as the boys had been by Massalia, they had no choice but to be amazed by this most incredible of places, and yet this was merely the gateway to the great city of Rome itself, less than a day's journey from here. As the ship slipped into harbour on the tide, huge grain ships from all over the world, some up to a hundred paces long and taking almost two weeks to unload fully, sat rocking gently in the swell as lines of slaves walked up and down the gangplanks like ants. As the ship docked, the boys watched a huge crane lifting a large stone. It was almost as big as the great stones that stood in a circle on the bleak plain to the north of their old village. The boys remembered a visit to the ancient monument built, it was said, by old Gods. Now no longer used, it was abandoned for the oak groves favoured by the Deru-Weidi. It took quite some time to tie up the ship and organize the gangplanks and, all the while, the boys watched the activity of the harbour with wonder. There were long ramps leading away from the quayside to warehouses and on to the open road. Much merchandise, particularly grain, was cross-loaded from the vast ships into smaller boats which would continue the journey, upriver, straight into the city itself. Many goods would be sold in Ostia, particularly slaves which were much needed for the labour intensive work of unloading. Still other loads, such as the boys' wagon, would continue by road to Rome. They disembarked amid much confusion and unnecessary pushing and pulling by the local dock workers. Blyth's mastery over the horses was total. They had to negotiate fees and complete documentation in a large building close to the docks. Gwenn had a contact, a citizen named Titus, who assisted with this before showing them to their lodging house and giving the boys a guided tour.

18

There was a lot of building work going on. There had been a battle only a few years earlier, when rival leaders fought over control of Rome; a consul and general named Marius had occupied Ostia and stolen much treasure. Repairs were still underway to damaged buildings, and new buildings were being added. Although there was not a full city wall there was a clear boundary fence, and gates at the southern and eastern ends of the town. In a Gallic or Pretanic town there was hardly a straight line anywhere. Here everything was a mass of straight lines and geometrical shapes. The boys had grown up with a way of life that worked with nature, using the shapes it provided and training it to provide what they needed. One of their greatest achievements was their use of wood. Trees were grown into specific shapes to serve specific purposes, a branch would be made to grow at the perfect angle, and all other branches were pruned from the trunk, to make a ship's prow. Trees were coppiced to produce perfect lengths of wood of exactly the right shape. The properties of different woods were all known and taught in folklore. A yew would be grown dead straight by carefully pruning out all side growth until it could be cut and split into quarters to make four perfect bows for hunting, trees were even grown in groups and plaited together to make shapes which defied belief, benches, and ladders, houses and temples could be constructed from groves of trees plaited together. It took patience, sympathy, and even love for the living wood, and a belief in the Gods that ruled over every part of life.

Here the Romans showed their absolute mastery over nature, by removing all trace of it from their cities: bricks and stone held together by mortar, to withstand the strongest wind or rain; rendered walls in searing white, not a crack permitted where a pioneering plant might find a foothold; uniform roof tiles in red terracotta, interlocked in military precision. There were warehouses and workshops, restaurants and shops, the market and the forum, temples to many different Gods, statues of white marble painted brightly and sometimes gilded, and mosaics in thousands of colours. The baths were particularly impressive; the boys had never considered bathing to get clean. They swam, of course, but when hunting they would often roll in the dung of their prey to mask their scent. Here, men and women went to scrub off every last natural smell and once again suppress nature in favour of human mastery. Murals painted on walls depicted everything from scenes of Gods and Goddesses to advertisements for the local bakery. The people were more uniform too, mostly Roman citizens wearing plain white tunics under plain togas; the slaves dressed almost the same, working away at various tasks or on errands for their masters. The wealthier citizens of the upper classes wore tunics with stripes on either side to denote their class: narrow stripes for the equestrian class and broader stripes for the senatorial class.

This was Man's world, where nature and the Gods were subservient to Mankind, but it was also a man's world, where women took a minor role in everything. Women did not participate in political life or military life; they looked after the home and hearth while men did all the 'important' work. Gwenn was frowned at by passing men as much as she attracted secretly admiring glances.

The culture of the Romani was alien to the boys who were so much a part of nature. There were hardly any plants, except in the courtyard gardens which were kept in perfect order, usually by slaves, the plants regimented to human will. Some of the narrower streets were impassable by wheeled vehicles, having large blocks of stone at intervals across the streets. Thermopolia thronged with people drinking mulled wine, eating fresh baked flat bread, and foods from every part of the world. After a lightning tour of the town and a quick snack at one of the many thermopolia they headed back to the port to see how Gwenn had got on. She was waiting for them when they arrived, and called out to them. A new ship had arrived from far away and was unloading a most exotic cargo.

A number of small cages were already stacked along a jetty. Inside them were a number of creatures the boys had never seen before. There were large and colourful birds in profusion, and a number of lizards, but what caught Abbon's attention were four cages each containing a creature like a small ugly child covered in black hair from head to toe. He sat by one of the cages looking at one of them. Its face was pink and its eyes were intelligent and melancholy and it had almost human-like hands and feet. Two dark shining eyes looked out at Abbon from a face that looked for all the world like it might be about to speak.

"Hello," Abbon said. The chimpanzee said nothing, so Abbon poked a finger through the bars, and almost lost it. The bleeding was quite bad but he kept quiet and stopped it with a piece of rag he had found.

"Alright, so you don't want to be friendly then," he added, a little bitterly, and then turned to see a large cage being lifted from the ship onto the dockside by one of the cranes used for heavy items. As he watched, the crane jerked and the cage slipped, dangling precariously twenty feet above the ground. There was a wave of panic around the dock from anyone who was close to being underneath. There was a pause before the whole cage slipped again, and fell crashing onto the ground. It broke open, and out walked the largest cat anyone had ever seen. It was about three paces long from nose to tail, with thick dark stripes on an orange coloured coat. Still a little shaken from the fall, it looked round with interest at all the unfamiliar prey before it. The prey scattered more or less immediately in every direction at once, slave and freeman alike, and the tiger's attention was drawn to one of the chimpanzees, which chose this moment to scream at random about its current condition. This drew the tiger's attention to Abbon who backed away terrified, but Gwenn, Blythe and Teague could all see that he had nowhere to go because he was trapped on a disused jetty where the cages had been stacked. The tiger advanced slowly and began to realize that this was going to be easy, he had caught prey like this once before in his own territory and it didn't fight back - small and helpless and very tender eating - his memories flooded back as he stalked, ever more quickly. Blyth and Teague threw stones and shouted but they were not going to put him off his meal; he had been bumped around and barely fed for days and wasn't going to miss out on this now. Abbon reached the edge of the pier and there was nowhere to go but into the turbid river below. He could swim a bit but there were strong currents and he could see nowhere to get back to shore. He held on to a rotten post which had been used to tie ships up. The tiger sped up a little more, it would not leap as it did not want to go over the edge either, and Abbon could see the whiskers and its dark tongue between rows of sharp teeth in its opening mouth as it loomed at him, and at that moment his foot slipped and the post fell away with him. He tumbled out of sight and a few moments later there was a splash. The tiger just managed to keep its footing and turned away from the edge of the pier where a new problem presented itself. A slave had been ordered to deal with the tiger, scared as he was he could not disobey his master, and there he stood with a fishing net and a three pronged fishing spear as his only defence. The crowd moved closer to watch the free entertainment, reasoning that even if the slave was unsuccessful he would slow the beast down for a while. Besides, they did not have to outrun a tiger, they only had to outrun someone else in the crowd.

The battle went the way mismatched battles of this type so often do, there was a brief period of sizing up the opponent, of parry and thrust, and then a mistake followed by a merciless strike. The slave made the mistake. He was no trained retiarius; he tripped over his own net, dropping the trident. The tiger struck with unerring accuracy, swiping four long slashes across the fallen man's chest before moving in for the kill. Gwenn had already dived into the river the moment Abbon fell and was swimming round searching for him. Teague, the quickest of the brothers, now grabbed the trident and got a hold of an edge of the netting, shouting at the tiger who turned on him. Teague stood his ground. Blyth told him to back away and get out of there, but

Teague stood firm and composed; his imagination had given him a reason to capture this magnificent beast and his dreams gave him focus. All the while he muttered prayers and spells to aid his chances. The tiger was impatient and this time he made the first mistake, he leapt at Teague who stepped back and held the trident to one side, pulling the net in front of him. The tiger's paws got entangled in the net and Teague quickly threw the remainder over the struggling creature, running round to make sure it stayed trapped.

"Kill it!" shouted Blyth, coming closer to try to help.

"No! He's MINE!" Teague screamed even louder.

Blyth managed to grab a coil of rope and come to help his brother, although he couldn't see why Teague had not finished the animal off at the first opportunity. As they trussed up the struggling tiger, scratched and bleeding as they were, the boys felt a strange kind of elation. A cheer went up from the crowd, now moving closer, and then from out of the press of bodies stepped a corpulent man wearing a white toga, and with a face that would have made an angry boar look attractive. He smiled a false smile and said, "Gratias vobis maximas ago. Quod meam mercem recuperastis. Hinc præerunt serui mei."

Blyth and Teague looked bewildered. Fortunately for the boys Gwenn reappeared from her search of the river. She made a strong impression on the crowds: dripping wet, in just a tunic, with a sword strapped to her leg by leather thongs and her platinum hair dripping with the river water as she climbed up to the jetty via a rickety ladder. She spoke in Latin to the merchant.

The slave lay dying close by as she spoke, and the attention of a well-meaning passer-by was not helping much. As he lay there he called out in a language the boys recognised, "Lugh, Lugh, I can see the light of your halls." Gwenn knelt down to him and whispered some words into his ear and he smiled one last painful smile before becoming still. Gwenn closed his eyes for him and he joined Lugh in the next life.

Gwenn turned her steely blue eyes on the merchant but kept one eye on the crowd. "Quomodo pueros remuneraberis pro cura eorum?" she said.

"What are you saying?" Teague called to her.

"He wants to take the animal back and he doesn't think he should have to pay you for catching it," she said, without turning her head.

"Tell him I want the animal," said Teague.

Gwenn glanced at him and raised an eyebrow before turning back to the merchant. "Feram tenebimus, pro cura."

"Minime!" replied the merchant.

Teague didn't know the words but he knew the tone of voice. "Unless you want me to let it go again?!" he shouted.

"Meus amicus dicit bestiam tibi ipsi capiendam esse, si eam habere vis," Gwenn explained.

"Qualis arrogantia! Tigris illa est mea!" retorted the merchant

"Tell him," said Teague, "I'll let it go right now unless he swears to let me keep it."

Gwenn relayed this to the merchant, although Teague cutting through a part of the net with his dagger needed little translation.

A number of people began to push backwards, trying to get further away, but quite a few blamed the merchant's stubbornness. A few felt that the young man had earned his prize for his courage in capturing the beast alive, and they began to voice their opinions in no uncertain terms.

The merchant for his part was unmoved by the argument but he was being rapidly moved, by the press of bodies around him, closer to the edge of the pier until he slipped - or was perhaps pushed - and fell into the river below.

The crowd, having no personal stake in events other than not wishing to be savaged by a tiger, parted in an unmistakable signal that the visitors should leave and take the tiger with them - the quicker the better. Some poles were found and some more fishing nets to carry the tiger. Led by the wet and glistening Gwenn, the boys were ushered on their way; the crowd giving them and the tiger a wide berth as they passed.

A contubernium arrived shortly afterwards but was sufficiently confused by all the conflicting stories that the boys were able to make a clean getaway, at least for the time being. The dead slave was removed and the merchant was rescued from the waters and eventually the soldiers were able to get his side of the story. The boys and Gwenn returned to their lodgings and made plans to leave early the next morning, but Teague had some unfinished business.

19

Back down at the dockside Teague waited in a dark alley and watched the pier where Abbon had fallen into the river. There was a soldier there who had been told to watch over the cages, which had not been moved to the warehouse yet due to the excitement of the day. The merchant had paid the Decanus handsomely to ensure the safety of his property and he was keen to do well.

Teague transformed into a cat and stalked through the shadows, silently slipping between the cages and the edge of the pier. The chimpanzees stirred a little in their sleep. Parrots ruffled feathers and tucked beaks into wings as he passed. Finally he found what he had suspected he would. Shivering with fear, was a squirrel hiding behind one of the cages. Teague sped between the cages and up behind the watching soldier transforming into his human self as he did so and pushing as hard as he could, the soldier, caught off balance, fell headlong into the river. "Come on Abbon," he called.

Abbon transformed to his human shape and called to Teague to help him.

"I want one of these," he said, pointing at the chimpanzee cages.

"We'll get caught," replied Teague.

"Then I'm not going," said Abbon stubbornly.

"Oh come ON then," Teague grumbled, and he grabbed one end of the nearest cage.

Together the two boys struggled into the shadows and then fled as quickly as possible back to the lodgings, with the shouts of soldiers behind them.

Their arrival back at the lodging was greeted with much emotion. Blyth was pleased to see his brother alive and well, but angry that he had not let them know he was safe. Gwenn was similarly pleased but worried that they had arrived in Roman lands without the veil of secrecy that she had hoped for.

Titus was beside himself with worry.

"You have to get out of here. There could be soldiers here any minute."

"Come on," said Gwenn. "Get all the stuff packed and let's get out of here before those soldiers come snooping round, asking questions."

"Sleep?" suggested Teague.

"Food?" enquired Abbon who had not eaten since their guided tour of the town.

"Later," Gwenn promised, "but first we have to get

out of here unless you want to end up on the menu at the arena."

They retrieved the horses and the wagon, and made to depart.

"There may be guards. You might be searched," warned Titus. "Word will have got around and you will be detained. They treat criminals harshly here."

"Then what can we do?" asked Gwenn.

"They are looking for three Celts with a tiger. I suggest you leave the tiger, I might be able to... I don't know... leave it somewhere where it can be found."

"We can't do that," said Teague.

"Why? What's so important about it?" asked Blyth. "You should have killed it when you had the chance. And what possessed you to bring that other thing back? If you'd left that and come back in your animal forms we might be able to wait until the morning; leave tomorrow."

"We need the animals alive," put in Abbon.

Realisation dawned on Gwenn first and Blyth shortly after.

"No!" they said, one after the other.

"Yes!" replied Abbon and Teague as one.

Gwenn thought hard and decided maybe they could try and bribe their way out.

"Get the wagon ready. Abbon, Teague, and I will transform. Titus will you drive the wagon?"

"It's very risky!" declared Titus.

"I know," soothed Gwenn. "I wouldn't ask if there

was any other way. Blyth can't speak Latin. If he is stopped he'll arouse suspicion immediately, but if he is with you, you can do all the talking."

"Will you make it worth my while?" enquired Titus.

"You can take all the tin from the cargo, it will fetch a good price at the market. Keep the dogs as well; too many people saw us arrive with them. Use the gold to bribe the soldiers but only the minimum it takes, otherwise you might look desperate. I'll sedate the animals, cover them with the hides. If bribery doesn't work, then as a last resort we'll use the element of surprise. Where can we go when we escape?"

"There is a forest and mountain to the east of here, south-east of Rome. It is sparsely populated, and there are plenty of places to hide out there."

"Right, if we get separated we head east and find each other later."

Blyth was nervous as he approached the gates, with Titus driving the little wagon.

They had done a good job of covering the tiger and chimpanzee, which were fast asleep and would stay that way until Gwenn wanted them awake. They took the main road to the Eastern gate. There was a guard but they did not pay much attention to the wagon; they had been told to look out for a tall woman and two boys. Blyth was wearing a toga and looked every bit the good apprentice next to Titus.

"Salvete!" called Titus as they reached the gates. There was a short exchange in Latin. Blyth kept his mouth shut and listened; it seemed to be going well - smiles and cheerfulness. He could tell they were talking about him, he heard the word 'puer' a few times, and the mood turned sombre. Luckily he maintained his complete silence, as Titus had told the guards that the boy could not speak but was a hard worker.

The legionary wanted to check the cargo but Titus told them he was in a hurry as he should have left hours ago, that he was heading for an inn on the way to Rome to meet someone and that he might lose a sale, which was going to make him a lot of money. He suggested perhaps he could share some of his good fortune with them if they would help him to go quickly. They took the hint and wondered what the merchant had to offer. He produced a small bag of coins which on closer inspection did little to impress the soldiers. They pointed out that a Decanus had been offered ten times that much to find some thieves and return a stolen tiger. Titus did a good impression of a merchant haggling over a deal and not happy with the way it was going. He grudgingly produced a larger bag, which seemed to do the trick. The gates were opened, but as the wagon rolled forward there was a shout from the end of the street. Then everything happened at once: a cat which had been watching from the top of the gate leapt onto the legionary's head and raced out, a squirrel followed and the wagon lumbered through the open gates before they could be closed. The wagon was swiftly followed by a huge white mare gleaming in the moonlight.

Two more legionaries arrived and told what had just happened at the docks. By the time there was any thought of giving chase the wagon was already quite some way down the road and since they would be pursuing on foot there was little they could do, at least for now.

The little wagon followed the road for some way and then the party struck off to the south-east using the stars to guide them, they reached some woodland after a few hours and disappeared into the trees.

"How am I going to go back now?" asked Titus. "I'll be recognized."

The dogs were at his apartment in Ostia with most of his possessions. He was not rich or from an old family, in fact his family were from Galatia, a land beyond Hellena, settled by Gallic people centuries before. His grandfather had been a mercenary and fought against Rome, alongside the Helleni. He was killed and his son, who was still a boy, was spared and sold as a slave to the captain of a merchant ship. He was freed after many years of service and settled in Ostia, where Titus was born a freeman and was, in truth, more Roman than Galatian, but his father taught him the stories and poems that he could remember, and Titus was fluent in Gallic and Greek, as well as Latin. He made a little money as a teacher, but with cheap slaves so readily available it was hard to make much.

"You still have the tin," Gwenn pointed out. "Lie low here for a bit and then buy some land down south, in Campania, or head for your family home in Galatia."

"Perhaps you are right," agreed Titus, with mixed emotions.

Blyth beat Titus to the next question. "So where are we staying tonight?"

"And what about food?" added Abbon.

Teague said nothing as he was already asleep, wrapped up in one of the furs.

"Well Titus, I guess we'll show you how the Galli live then." Gwen said with a wicked grin.

"Hey you're not going to do any human sacrifices are you? I've heard stories."

"Ha ha, that's very funny Titus; your grandfather would be ashamed of you," replied Gwenn. "Coming from someone who is happy to watch men fight to the death for sport!" she added, walking a line between joking and seriousness.

"Hey, I hardly ever go to those things! But you can't tell me the Keltoi are a peace loving people; you lot would kill for a bone!"

"Hey let's not fight shall we? How long have we known each other? Tell me if you still think we are barbarians in the morning."

Gwenn stopped the wagon and jumped down. "This looks like a good place."

"There's nothing but trees!" exclaimed Titus.

"That's all we need," said Blyth.

There was a circle of young trees, each about twice the height of a man. Gwenn walked around these in a large circle, muttering under her breath. The trees grew fairly straight, around a rotten stump, racing each other to reach the canopy. Blyth got some rope and Abbon climbed one of the trees and threw the rope across to the one opposite. He tied off one end of the rope and then climbed down, and up the next tree. Within a few minutes they had pulled all the tree tops down to a central point and tied them off using the rope. They wove the tree branches into each other creating a loose upside down basket. Meanwhile Blyth and Gwenn had collected quite a lot of straight sticks and bracken which they used to make a rough covering of the rest of the structure. They cheated a bit, secretly using magic to waterproof the loosely woven material and they threw plenty of furs down around the inside. When Titus wasn't looking, Gwenn conjured a fire using magic, and they settled down to a feast of bread and dried meat.

Titus had to admit that they were warm and dry and reasonably comfortable but he could see that a bath was some way off and there was little to do for entertainment. However, after some of Teague's tea he had no use for either as he was sleeping soundly on a pile of furs within moments of putting the cup down.

Teague was first to wake, with the dawn, and Gwenn moments later. They brewed up for morning tea and woke the rest of the party. Titus yawned, stretched and took in his surroundings. His expression said more than words but Gwenn, silently, thrust a steaming hot cup of morning tea into his hands and he sipped. As they sipped they began to chat and Titus admitted that he had slept soundly and that he was comfortable, but that he needed a bath.

"I think there might be a river to the east," said Blyth.

"I could check," said Abbon. "It wouldn't take long."

"I was thinking more of a proper bath with steam rooms and hot and cold plunge pools?"

"Well we can't stay here forever," said Gwenn. "Any ideas about entering Rome without looking suspicious?"

"Well I'd say not having a bloody great tiger and a chimpanzee with us might come in handy," Titus exclaimed, with a touch of irony.

"If I understand my brothers correctly that won't be a problem after the next new moon?" Blyth directed his question at Teague and Abbon.

"Which is in just over a fortnight," murmured Gwenn.

"Around the calends. Two weeks without a bath," muttered Titus. "Two weeks!"

"We'll sort something out," assured Gwenn.

20

Later that day they hunted, but Gwenn did not use magic; she wasn't at all sure they could trust Titus enough to risk him seeing it. He was not Deru-Weido, nor even truly Gallic. He was just her best contact in Ostia and nothing more. He was obviously used to the creature comforts of Roman life and might easily betray them for enough money. Gwenn did however keep her eyes open for certain plants that she thought might be useful, not just for food. One little purple flower got her very excited. It was growing under a hedge near a path. It had tall dark stems and spearhead-shaped leaves. At about knee height, there was a cluster of delicate lilac flowers, each with five petals. Gwenn dug the plants up and kept the lumpy roots, and the leaves.

Teague and Abbon went on ahead and helped to flush out game. With the spell protecting the camp, no-one but them could see the hut or surrounding area, unless they walked right into it, which Gwenn felt was reasonably unlikely. They cooked roast boar and herbs and vegetables. They drank herbal teas and a little wine from their small store. Teague and Abbon went on scouting sorties and came back with stories of patrols on the roads and legionaries searching the villas and settlements all over the area.

Meanwhile Titus continued to teach Blyth Latin and Blyth taught Titus the rudiments of Teague's game. It had been a while since Blyth had played because he didn't like losing to Teague, which almost always happened. Gwenn watched; she had learned the game from Trethiwr, and she was able to correct Blyth on one or two points of the rules. As Blyth took a commanding lead she made a couple of suggestions to help Titus out, but not too much, so that Blyth was able to claim a victory. Later, Teague played Gwenn and was disappointed to be able to defeat her easily.

They found a river which bubbled up from the ground and filled a number of indentations of varying sizes in the dark rock, as it tumbled away down the slopes. Since the weather was exceptionally warm for the spring and the dark rock concentrated the sun's heat into the water, the smaller pools were surprisingly warm. Gwenn had chopped up the roots and leaves of the purple-flowered plant that she had collected previously, and boiled them in water to produce a liquid soap.

They were able to splash reasonably hot water on

their faces from the smallest pools, and Titus even managed something like a decent shave. Some pools were large enough to submerge in lukewarm water. The river itself was almost freezing, while any areas of flat black rock, exposed to the sun, were almost too hot to touch.

As they lay basking in the warm sun a tinkling sound warned them of the approach of a herd of goats. They quickly gathered up their things and got out of sight. Teague and Abbon darted into the woods to hide. Gwenn, Titus, and Blyth composed themselves and relaxed in the warm sunshine. The boy was about Teague's age, driving a dozen or so goats along the path.

"Salve," called Titus.

They exchanged greetings and idle chat about the weather.

The boy asked where they were from, and they told him they had come from Campania to visit friends, which the boy seemed to accept.

Titus asked if there was any news and the boy told them that someone called Calpurnia had given birth to a boy, and both mother and baby were doing well. He confided that a man named Marcus Valerius had accused his neighbour Lucius Spurius of damaging his property, but that he himself had seen Valerius do the damage.

"I'm not going to say anything though. Better not to get involved," the boy added.

"Anything from Rome or Ostia?" enquired Titus.

"Nothing much. A couple of thieves left the port in a hurry after stealing some goods, but they reckon they will have a hard time of it. The story is they stole a huge wild cat, as big as a horse, and the only place they can sell it is at the arena in Rome. If it hasn't eaten them already. As long as it doesn't escape around here, it's not my problem."

And so, the goat herd went on his way, leaving Teague and Abbon to re-emerge from the trees and for Gwenn to fill them in on the details.

"Well we won't be able to sell your tiger, or the chimpanzee, boys," joked Gwenn.

"Not after we've finished with them we won't," was Teague's macabre response.

Gwenn and Titus spent the time they had teaching the boys as much Latin as they could get them to learn. They were going to need it if they were to spend any time in Rome.

"Romans don't trust strangers, no matter where they are from," explained Titus. "Allies and subject states of the Republic are protected in law; their status is 'hospitium', which allows them to conduct business and move freely without fear of hindrance. Citizens of enemies are declared 'hostis', and may be arrested and either sold into slavery or executed. Any other stranger is called a barbarian and they are feared and mistrusted. The law does little to protect them and they might be kidnapped and sold into slavery by an unscrupulous trader."

The boys listened carefully to this and concentrated hard on learning the language. Learning things like poetry and stories was a big part of Deru-Weidi training so it wasn't so difficult for them.

"If you can learn enough to get by, you could claim to be Salluvi or Voconti from Gallia Narbonensis. Nobody will expect you to be perfect, as long as you are making the effort, that way you will be entitled to hospitium."

Luckily, languages seemed to come naturally to Blyth, which made him feel that, here at least, he was superior to his brothers. He delighted in discovering that some words were the same but with perhaps one consonant change. Before long, Blyth could guess at many words on the first hearing, and was soon insisting on speaking nothing but Latin.

They returned to the spring a few times and Titus, with Gwenn's help, persuaded Blyth to shave and cut his hair so that he might fit in better in Rome. Titus told them that they simply had to visit the baths when they reached Rome and then they would see how a proper bath should be.

Eventually the day of the new moon arrived and as the sun set the two younger boys went with Gwenn to a clearing they had spotted a few days earlier. It was mainly surrounded by oaks with a few other trees but it was good enough in Gwenn's judgement and the ceremony was carried out at midnight according to the ritual. Blyth waited with Titus, at the camp, in uncomfortable silence. Titus was wary of Gwenn and had a natural Roman mistrust of foreigners, but he suppressed this because of his affection for Gwenn. Gwenn, for her part, showed no interest in Titus in that way, but that didn't dim his interest.

"How do you come to know Gwenn?" asked Blyth.

"She comes and goes. The first time I saw her I was walking along the harbour side. She was standing on the prow a ship coming into the port. She looked stunning; the wind blew her hair, like the white tips of waves breaking on the shore, and her eyes shone bluer than the sky, but she stood as solid as a marble statue. I watched her right up to the point where I walked into a beam, and everything went black."

Blyth laughed, on cue. When they had both stopped laughing Titus continued, "Next thing, I'm waking up with her holding my head in her arms and I thought I'd gone to the afterlife of my grandfather. She looks like a goddess," he uttered dreamily.

Blyth coughed, embarrassed. He was beginning to have similar feelings about Gwenn after the scene at the docks, but he had also dreamed a fair bit about Blodwyth lately. The two men sat by the fire, playing the battle game and sipping hot tea, waiting for the return of their friends.

Eventually they heard an ethereal cry, like a cross between a newborn baby's first scream and an old woman's laugh. It rang out across the forest and was followed by a deep throated roar that resonated through the air like the war cry of a thousand men. Blyth and Titus shivered at the strange sounds. For Blyth, knowing that this was only his little brothers changing into a chimpanzee and a tiger didn't help much. Both men felt tingles crawling up their spines, every hair on end.

There was silence for what seemed like a long time and then the light tread of people used to moving quietly in a forest approached the round hut. The furs across the entrance were pulled aside and Teague followed Abbon into the gloomy interior. Gwenn ducked in after them, but little was said. Titus suspected something strange had been going on but he didn't want to know. Blyth conceded defeat in the current game with Titus, and drank some sleep tea. Teague and Abbon whispered a lot and Gwenn gave one ear to them and one eye to the young man who was so like Trethiwr in so many ways.

Sleep overtook them and the sun was high in the sky before there was any movement in the hut.

21

On the morning of the next day they struck camp, releasing the living trees which had formed the framework of their home and spreading the bracken and loose branches around the area. The fire was put out and the ashes buried and covered with leaf litter. If anyone but a very observant hunter were to pass by here they would never suspect that it had been home to five people for over a week. Titus had decided to head south for Campania before deciding his next move. Gwenn suggested that he should take the wagon with the tin and hides as it would draw attention to them now. She also reasoned that he would be less likely to sell them out to the authorities if he had enough to set himself up in another area. They parted company when they reached the Via Appia, Titus heading southwards, towards Pompeii, Gwenn and the boys, north towards the great city of Rome.

As they drew near to the city there were strange-looking stone buildings. Some were quite small, others were almost as large as a house, with steps leading down to heavy doors. Gwenn explained that these were graves, where the ashes of family members were placed. Seeing the city from a distance they marvelled at its size. All villages in Pretan were built at the top of hills; this city was spread across a whole series of hills, with the river running along one side. It was surrounded by a huge wall at least three times the height of a man and thicker than the span of Blyth's arms. They entered via the arch of the Porta Capena.

The sheer scale of the architecture was overwhelming; people lived in tall buildings, called insulae, divided into small dwellings. Temples - there were several - had rows of gleaming white columns and ornate carvings on the sides. The forum alone was almost bigger than the boys' whole village. They did not know where to look next as there was so much going on.

Gwenn led the way to a large taverna with stables at the back for the horses. Once the animals had fresh hay and water, Gwenn and the boys found rooms and had something to eat and drink. The taverna owner gave them some funny looks but accepted their story of being wealthy Salluvi. They certainly wore enough gold and carried enough money to suggest the truth of their story.

Over the next few days they visited the baths and

marvelled at the facilities. They watched the chariot races, which Blyth insisted he would have won easily had he been at the reins, and they walked for what seemed like miles around the markets, amazed at the variety of goods on offer.

On one visit to the baths Blyth met a young man of about the same age as himself; he was slim and pale with dark hair and dark eyes. He introduced himself as Caius Julius Caesar and asked where Blyth was from. Blyth told him he was a Salluvi warrior, which seemed to be accepted. The young man questioned him at length about his tribe, his customs, and beliefs. He asked about rumours he had heard that they burned people alive and told fortunes by cutting out the stomachs of living captives. Blyth played this down although he was well aware that these things were sometimes done, out of necessity. He also pointed out that it was not so different from the games where criminals were killed by wild animals. But he thought of his own father who he had seen savagely killed just two years ago, and he faltered.

"Are you alright?" asked the Roman.

"I was thinking of my father; he died two years ago," replied Blyth, omitting details of the savagery of his execution.

"Then we have something in common. My father died not long ago as well. He was putting on his shoes and he just… died," he said it with as much puzzlement as sadness. "How old are you?" he asked Blyth.

"I am sixteen in a few months."

"I will be sixteen in a few months and I am the Paterfamilias. Are you the head of your household now?" he asked Blyth.

"My mother is still alive," responded Blyth. "She went to... " Blyth hesitated as he had been about to say that she had gone to the lands of the Iceni in the East of Pretan when he remembered he was supposed to be a Salluvi warrior from Gallia Narbonensis.

The Roman youth interrupted him, "So when exactly are you sixteen?"

The question was not a simple one since the two boys used completely different calendars. Eventually, after much discussion, they agreed that they must have been born on, or very nearly on, the same day.

At this point some other men came in who knew the youth and he was drawn into their circle, leaving Blyth with his thoughts. His main thought was that being beaten, strangled, stabbed, and left face down in a bog, was not very similar to falling down dead while putting on a pair of shoes, but it was too late to make that point now. The other thought creeping over him was that his father had said that his life was inextricably tied up with the life of a boy who was born on the same day. He was said to be associated with wolves. But that did not make any sense so Blyth decided to forget about it.

About a week into their stay the boys were in the taverna sipping wine. Gwenn was otherwise occupied;

she often went off to meet up with people and organize things. Blyth was being moody and arguing with his brothers, Teague was trying to convince him that he should try to learn to transform into an animal and Blyth was stonewalling as usual. Eventually he lost his temper completely and stood up abruptly, knocking the table away as he did so and spilling wine all over the floor. He stormed out into the night. Abbon called after him but Teague told Abbon to leave him and let him simmer down. When Gwenn arrived back she was immediately worried. Blyth had not come back and she knew he was so hot headed that he could easily get into trouble. She ordered Abbon and Teague to go to the room and not let anyone in until she returned. Then she went back into the night to search for Blyth.

Blyth did not have any idea where he was going after storming out of the taverna. All he knew was he wanted to get away and have some quiet time alone. Unfortunately he soon ran into trouble of a more serious nature. He was walking quickly, blindly, filled with pent-up anger. As he dashed around a corner he ran bodily into a big burly man accompanied by another seven men, a contubernium of legionaries, off duty and heading for the taverna. He bounced off the man's barrel chest and landed on the floor but his mouth recovered quickly and he cursed the man in his own language, the language of the Dwr-Y-Tryges.

"What do we have here?" said the Decurion. "It's a barbarian invasion lads!"

Accompanied by laughter from his comrades, he picked Blyth up by the front of his clothes and gave the command for a defensive formation. More laughter. Blyth was apoplectic and a red mist came down, he kicked out, catching the Decurion right between the legs. The soldier let him go and went down on his knees; Blyth froze for a second and then ran. The remaining soldiers gave chase and quickly caught him, dragging him back to their fallen Decurion. "Beat him," he ordered.

The legionaries threw Blyth down face first, and kicked him repeatedly until he passed into unconsciousness. The Decurion issued the last kick and then hobbled away, leaving Blyth to his fate. He lay there for about an hour unconscious, and as he lay he dreamed a strange dream. He was a wolf and he was running, running for his life. Surrounding him were other wolves, chasing him. As hard as he ran they kept pace with him easily. When he turned, they turned with him. His desperate flight seemed to go on for a long time. He felt himself being dragged back, slowed down, caught by trees, wallowing in mud, and the wolves were closing in. Then he was flying, flying over the trees and the rivers and the hills away over the glittering sea and into white mountains. He felt himself being lowered onto a cliff edge, he could feel the hard rock under his back and his head.

Eventually he began to return to consciousness, on the hard stone pavement. But even as he tried to sit up, with every muscle screaming agony at him, a man came around the corner wearing dark robes and moving silently.

"What's this then?" the voice was rough. The speaker was already calculating where the best profit lay in this situation.

Expert eyes appraised Blyth from his plain tunic and toga to the spread of pale stubble on his chin and decided he was not of high status. He eyed the gold torc around his neck and surmised that he was a Gaul and therefore an easy target. He grabbed at the torc but Blyth tried to stop him. The man kicked him and Blyth's head hit the ground and he fell unconscious once more. Quickly the thief found a purse of money and ripped it from Blyth's neck, taking his arm torcs as well. Blyth's head oozed blood where it had hit the stone and the thief decided that the body should be found elsewhere. He dragged Blyth to a rougher part of the city where he dumped him in a dark corner before disappearing into the night.

22

Gwenn searched the streets and asked the few passers-by that she met if they had seen him. A group of legionaries informed her that they had seen him a few streets away but that he was hurt. "Why didn't you help him?" she asked.

"I'm not a physician," protested the Decurion. "Besides he didn't seem to appreciate our efforts did he lads?" At this they laughed and Gwenn worried considerably more.

She hurried away in the direction they pointed, but by the time she reached where he had lain he was already several streets away and bleeding slowly into the dust.

Blyth lay outside the entrance to one of the insulae in a poor part of the city and the first resident who came out the next morning practically tripped over him. He was pale and weak but still alive when a slightly chubby merchant named Servius found him. The merchant lifted him and took him inside to his apartment. It was one of the better ones, on a lower floor, although it was still small. Servius called to his wife and instructed her to care for the youth, then he went off to open his shop in the marketplace.

On his return in the evening Blyth was sitting upright sipping a drink and although still very bruised he was at least conscious.

"Thank you for helping me," Blyth mumbled, his accent giving him away as a visitor.

"What happened to you?" enquired Servius.

"I was beaten by some men, then I remember waking up and another man stole my money. Then the next thing I knew I woke up here."

"Stole your money, eh?"

"If I can get back to my friends, I can pay you a reward for helping me," suggested Blyth.

"Perhaps, perhaps. Where are your friends?"

"They are staying at a taverna near the Porta Capena."

"If you feel alright we can go there right now; it's not too late."

The merchant led the way with Blyth following. But as they walked along the road Blyth spotted one of the soldiers who had attacked him the day before. He was laughing at something unconnected with Blyth, but the blood rose in the young Celt. He grabbed a pole that was supporting an awning and swung it across the back of the soldier's head, knocking him flat on his face.

Another soldier emerged from a doorway and Blyth caught him in the face before being wrestled to the ground by several more men. A large group of spectators gathered to watch, a few briefly cheering on the young lad who was obviously outmatched.

Once he was overpowered he was forced into a kneeling position, his arms held stretched out tightly on either side. His tunic was ripped from his back and the Decurion beat him with a stick until his back bled. After this short sharp shock a man in a toga stepped forward and raised a hand to prevent any more blows.

"I think perhaps I should take over from here, Decurion."

The Decurion recognised Publius Servilius Vatia, praetor. Even if he had not, the broad stripe on his toga and tunic would have indicated his rank surely enough.

"Of course, praetor," he deferred.

However, now another man expressed an interest. He wore a plain toga and had a chubby red face. Had Blyth been able to look up he would have recognised the face of the merchant from Ostia.

"This is one of the boys who stole my goods in Ostia," the merchant announced. "He owes a debt to me. I have just delivered a cargo of wild animals for the games here at the forum. Thanks to that young man and his brothers, my delivery was short by one tiger and one chimpanzee. He is a savage from Britannia, an enemy and a common criminal. There are games starting in the next hour and since we are missing some animals, let us make up the numbers with him."

"Very well," agreed the magistrate, "tie him up."

Blyth was beaten, bloodied and weak, but his ordeal was not over yet. His hands and feet were tied and he was dragged through the streets to the forum boarium, where the games were taking place.

Above the scene, watching from the rooftops, was a squirrel. It scampered along the apex of a roof and leapt from one building to another, watching to see where Blyth was taken. There was a simple building on one side of the forum in which about half a dozen criminals were locked up awaiting execution. A heavy wooden door was opened and Blyth was thrown inside, still tied up. In an area in the middle of the square was a large enclosure. Leading away from this there was a kind of tunnel which connected to the area where a number of animals were held captive. There was a bear, and several wolves, and other strange creatures, such as a huge sandy-coloured beast, like a giant cat, with a shaggy coat of darker hair around its face and neck, great sharp teeth in its gaping mouth and razor sharp claws. Another cat had dark spots on a pale coloured fur. None of them looked friendly.

As soon as Blyth was locked up and left alone, the squirrel scampered away.

A few minutes later the squirrel spotted a feral cat slinking along an alley and leapt down to it. The two animals went into a dark doorway and Teague and Abbon emerged shortly afterwards. From there they quickly found Gwenn and the three of them hatched a plan.

Within the hour Teague appeared in the forum square and walked nonchalantly towards the prisoners. He appeared to try and release the lock on the door but was soon spotted and the guard shouted a warning at him. The merchant appeared quickly afterwards and cried out, pointing at Teague. Immediately Teague ran off, leaving Blyth wondering what on earth the plan had been. How could Teague possibly expect to rescue him and get away from the middle of the forum? Teague disappeared round a corner, followed by the guards. When the guards came around the corner there was no sign of Teague; there was however a litter on which was a cage containing a full grown male tiger.

So the boy had apparently escaped but now they had recovered the tiger. Well he had seriously underestimated them. Smiling and laughing the two guards picked up the litter and carried the tiger back to the forum. The merchant and his customer were extremely pleased.

"How very appropriate. Now we can feed the Briton to the tiger that he stole!" laughed the organiser of the games.

As the sun reached the highest point in the sky the games began with the executions. Two Nubian slaves were thrown into the enclosure and their ties cut. From another gate two men entered armed with tridents and nets. An announcer explained in a booming voice that these slaves had been caught trying to steal a fishing boat in Ostia. It was therefore thought appropriate that they should be killed by retiarii. The two fighters approached their cowering, quivering victims with tridents raised and nets at the ready. The slaves offered no fight at all and were dispatched fairly quickly, much to the crowd's disappointment. The next victims – a woman and a boy of ten or twelve years old - were brought in and the lion was released. It waited what seemed like an eternity as the woman screamed at it, trying to protect her child behind her but then it ran and leapt onto her, grabbing her shoulder in its huge jaws. The boy was knocked aside but jumped up and hammered his fists onto the side of the great cat, screaming non-stop at the top of his voice, but with little effect. As soon as the mother's body had gone limp the lion turned and swiped a vast paw at the child, tearing his stomach open and silencing him for ever. It took a little while to clear the enclosure for the next execution. After all the other prisoners had been killed by a variety of gruesome methods, Blyth was thrown into the enclosure and his bonds cut.

Then the announcer explained that this savage, all the way from Britannia, had been caught stealing a tiger and trying to attack a group of soldiers. He then went on to tell them that the tiger had been recovered and so it was appropriate that the criminal would be killed by that tiger. The events that unfolded after the announcer left the arena were very confusing, especially for the

Roman citizens who witnessed what happened.

The tiger was released and it prowled slowly into the arena. Blyth tried to stand but he was weak from all the abuse his body had received; he had not been fed either, or even given a drink, and his eyes could barely focus.

The tiger walked slowly round him and glanced occasionally at the spectators from time to time. In the audience there was a tall woman wearing a white palla with a shawl over her head. On a rooftop at one side of the square there was a squirrel, keeping remarkably still. Nobody noticed the squirrel skitter down the slope of the roof and race across an open part of the square towards the enclosure. Then, seemingly from out of nowhere, a large chimpanzee bounded into the guard at the gate, then crashed at the gate itself knocking the latch and opening it. Another guard raced over but soon turned and fled as the tiger leapt through the gate. The chimp rushed off screaming and the crowd also fled in panic, clearing the forum in a surprisingly short time. Only one member of the crowd headed towards the enclosure; it was the woman with the shawl. In the confusion, nobody saw where the white horse came from. Blyth managed to struggle up onto the horse's back and raced out of the forum, closely followed by the tiger. The strange cavalcade raced down the street heading for the nearest gate, close to the river. The gates were open and the tiger appeared first, bounding towards the soldiers guarding it. They stepped back, swords drawn, unsure of how to respond, and the white horse raced past them before they had formed any kind of plan.

When they finally reacted they looked out towards the river to see the white horse and two others crossing the river, with a boy riding each. They couldn't see a tiger but they didn't go rushing out, just in case it was lurking somewhere nearby.

Before the Romans could give chase the Celts had melted into the scenery and gone.

23

They had escaped from the crowd but their problems were however far from over. Blyth was weak from all his injuries. He had cuts and bruises, and had not eaten properly for days. He coughed up blood a few times as well.

As soon as the immediate danger was over, Gwenn made them stop and she treated Blyth's wounds. He was still sick and would take some time to get better, but the worst was over. Gwenn insisted that the boys stay in their human forms unless there was immediate danger. She didn't want them to forget who they were or waste their powers. She was also worried that they had not done all the preliminary studies of animal behaviour for their new transformations.

And so they walked, under cover of woodlands wherever possible, keeping off the excellent Roman road except when they needed to cross it. The road was the Via Aurelia following the coast northwards towards Gaul. Gwenn reckoned that if they walked most of the way, and rode when it was safe to do so, they could be back in her village in fourteen nights.

Three days after leaving Rome they were in Pisae, where they narrowly evaded a patrol. Three days after that they were close to the skirted Mediolanum, carefully keeping an eye out for Roman soldiers and avoiding people wherever possible. They travelled by night and hid in woods, or whatever shelter they could find, during the day.

Then, as they began to ascend into the foothills of the Alps, they were spotted by a group of soldiers, including mounted auxiliaries. The soldiers recognised them from descriptions that had been circulated and immediately began to give chase. Unable to transform in sight of the soldiers the four mounted their two horses, Gwenn and Abbon on one and Blyth and Teague on the other, and rode as hard as they could for the cover of the mountains proper. There was a spur of rock and a lake. The route curved round the spur and if they could reach that before they were caught they could transform, and Blyth could ride his horse faster than any mounted soldier.

The auxiliaries were gaining on them and it was a close thing whether they could get out of sight before they were caught. The horses' muscles rippled with the effort and their breath curled in wreaths of mist in the cold dry air. Gwenn risked a brief backward glance and could see the sun glint off spear tips as they passed behind the spur. Hearts racing, sweat pouring off them, the horses' breath painting the air in clouds, there wasn't a moment to lose. Abbon transformed into the squirrel and skittered up the nearest tree. Gwenn quickly saw the danger in leaving him there and told him to jump onto her back, as she transformed once again into the snow white mare. Teague turned into a wildcat and raced off up the path heading further into the mountains. Blyth rode his magnificent horse and, with the other horses now riderless, they rode swiftly away from the chasing soldiers who even now rounded the spur into sight.

Confused at seeing what looked like one boy and two riderless horses disappearing from view they stopped to search for the remaining people who they presumed must have dismounted. After putting a considerable distance between themselves and the chasing soldiers, the four regrouped and transformed. Blyth was still tired and weak from his ordeal and wanted to rest. Gwenn was still worried that the soldiers would continue their chase. She did not want a confrontation with them.

Eventually she agreed to stop and rest for a while but told them to remain ready to leave at a moment's notice. She told Abbon and Teague to scout around and see if they could spot the soldiers. As a cat and a squirrel they would not attract any attention. Gwenn spent some time scratching on her wax tablet, before smiling quietly to herself. Teague came back a little while later, with

Abbon, and told Gwenn that they had seen the auxiliaries, apparently waiting for the rest of the soldiers to catch up. Gwenn gazed northwards across the lake where they had stopped, and pointed to a dark speck growing larger in the sky.

"Here he comes," she said.

As the speck grew larger they thought at first it was an eagle or a kite, but it continued to grow larger still, until they could make out a red leathery creature with a long neck and tail, and soon saw that it was being ridden by their Great Grandfather, Kaito. As the dragon skimmed low over the lake it was reflected gloriously, appearing to be flying both above and below the water, as if it occupied this world and the next at the same time. It landed, slightly clumsily, a short distance from the group of boys and Kaito leapt from its back like a puppy and embraced Gwenn.

Quickly Gwenn took control, commanding the boys and Kaito to mount the dragon while she would take the horses overland. She ordered them to hurry as the soldiers would soon catch up with them and could not be allowed to see the dragon. They wasted no time in clambering onto the large back, sitting between the horns that ran down its ridge and holding on for dear life as the dragon stretched its wings out, bringing them down with a thunderous clap and lifting off as awkwardly as it had landed. Once aloft it required just a few strokes of its massive wings to get high into the blue sky and it was a mere speck in the distance as the soldiers finally reached the place where the boys had been. The horses were now riderless, all three of them galloping fast and free, their manes streaming in the crisp mountain air up the valley beside the lake and out of sight once more.

It was still a long journey for Gwenn through the mountains to get back to her home village of Entwalen-Dun, but the weather was being kind now and Bellenos smiled undimmed all day. The nights were cold but since they travelled, with only occasional stops, by both day and night it mattered little.

Kaito landed the dragon high in the mountains some distance from Entwalen-Dun because he knew that ordinary people were never really comfortable around dragons. It would be better if they did not even know dragons existed - better for them and certainly better for the dragons.

He sent Teague and Abbon ahead with instructions. Abbon was to remain in the village and make sure that there would be food and drink for Blyth. Teague was to bring horses for the three of them. Soon Blyth was tucked up in a hut wrapped in furs and sipping special tea made by Teague. It would be several days before he was properly up and about, but then again it would be several days before Gwenn arrived back. This gave Blyth enough time to reflect on his recent adventures and the fact that if it had not been for Gwenn, and his brothers, and their ability to transform into wild animals, then he would not be alive now.

Gwenn arrived just in time for Belotenios so there was already a celebration in the village, which was all the better for the return of good friends and family. The feast was another impressive affair and a most welcome event after Blyth's ordeals. The boys became the centre of attention as they regaled the villagers with stories of the towns and cities they had visited, and of how Blyth faced down a raging stallion and tamed it. Blyth showed off the magnificent beast and no-one, not even the strongest warrior, remained unimpressed. Gwenn told of how Teague fought a ferocious cat. Hardly anyone believed her description of how big it was, but since she exaggerated significantly in the retelling of the story, the size they imagined was quite close to reality anyway. They laughed at the stories of the weak Romans who had to bathe every day, and who seemed to fall into the harbour with alarming regularity. They were shocked at the barbaric behaviour of the Roman warriors who would attack an innocent young man and beat him while he had no weapon to defend himself. But the worst shock was at the treatment of criminals: that they were sent unarmed into an arena and torn limb from limb by wild animals was unspeakably wrong. Trial by combat was understood, but the accused had to have a fair chance of winning. The Romani were savages, worse than wild animals; they had the ability to create beautiful buildings, and statues, they had the discipline to form large armies, and yet they had none of the civilisation of the kind and honest Keltoi.

After the feast, Blyth asked Gwenn if he could speak privately with her. When they were alone he said, "I'm ready to learn the transformation spell if you are still willing to teach me."

"Of course I am willing. I think there is nothing more important in fulfilling your father's prophesy."

"You know the animal I want to transform into?" he asked.

"There is only one that makes any sense. A wolf."

Blyth smiled and breathed a sigh of relief. It was nice when people understood him, without him having to say everything in words.

So all that summer, Blyth observed the behaviour of wolves. He and Gwenn tracked a large and dominant pack in the hills to the north of Entwalen-Dun. They built a hide in the branches of an ancient oak tree close to the centre of the pack's territory, with a large clearing close by, and Blyth spent almost all day, every day, there. Often the wolves would spend long stretches of the day right beneath him, the cubs tumbling over each other and their mothers in play, learning the moves they would later employ in hunting. He was not afraid of the wolves, and the more he understood them the braver he became.

Once, he was walking towards the hide early in the morning, when he realised that there was a wolf quite close by. He waited, to avoid giving away the position of the hide. The wolf paced, and sniffed the air, but was clearly more afraid of him than he was of it. Blyth sat down beside a tree. The wolf was young, not a fubsy downy cub that would stay very close to its mother for protection, yet young enough that it would not have made its first kill yet. Blyth leaned forward on his hands and knees and put his head close to the ground as he had seen the wolves do, and the wolf came closer. It too bent its body down low at the front, and Blyth shuffled closer forward, lifting his head then dropping it down. The wolf repeated the motion and was now close enough to sniff at Blyth's face. Blyth lifted his right hand and cuffed the wolf across the neck pushing it sideways. The wolf responded by lifting its paws in retaliation and turning his head to try and nip Blyth's hand. Blyth moved his hand quickly, and cuffed with the left then, as the wolf responded to that movement by pushing right, Blyth used his right hand to push the wolf down on its side. The young wolf rolled right over, trying still to bite Blyth's hands as they moved quickly, to stroke and avoid being bitten. The wolf drew blood and Blyth yelped slightly, but carried on playing as the wolf writhed about on its back.

Then there was a howl in the distance and the wolf twisted its body wildly to regain its footing. Blyth looked up in the direction of the howl, which came again, and the wolf bounded off without a second glance. Blyth took the opportunity to climb up to his hide in the tree and waited. Much later that day, the rest of the pack emerged in the clearing after their successful hunt.

24

Lughunasath came and went and the New Year loomed; Gwenn suggested that Blyth should take advantage of the New Year's new moon to conduct the ceremony to make his transformation. At the half moon before Samonios therefore, the two went out into the woods in search of a suitable wolf specimen to sacrifice for the ceremony. The first night brought nothing, but on the second night a young male walked calmly into the charmed area that Gwenn had set up. She indicated to Blyth that it was ideal but he looked unhappy. It was the same wolf that he had played with in the clearing and he didn't want to hurt it.

"Not that one," he whispered.

"Why not?"

"He's a... friend." Blyth had the decency to look embarrassed, but Gwenn did not question it. She pointed her staff and the merest rustle of air removed the spell. The charmed wolf seemed to wake up and simply trotted on without any apparent harm.

"It's not a problem," said Gwenn. "Remember Teague couldn't use the cats that I caught for him? Ideally it should be a fully wild animal that you haven't had contact with. So let's leave it for tonight and try again tomorrow."

The next night another, older, larger male wolf sauntered into the charmed area but was quickly joined by a female and another young wolf. This gave Gwenn a problem and again she broke the charm and they left it for another try. On the following night they travelled a lot further north, hoping to find a different range. This time they got what they wanted. A huge dark grey wolf stalked into the charmed area with the assurance of one who has nothing to fear.

Blyth had never seen such a magnificent beast. It seemed to be a lone wolf, alone out of choice, not rejection: much like Blyth. Its thick coat faded from mid grey to almost pure black on the ridge of its back. Amber eyes stared vacantly into the middle distance under the charm of the circle, but behind them there was a burning intelligence. Blyth offered a silent prayer asking the Gods for forgiveness for taking the life of such a fabulous beast, but he knew this was the one.

He and Gwenn slipped a strong bag over the beast and quickly tied it tightly before slinging it on a pole for the long walk back to Entwalen-Dun. There the wolf was placed into a cage where it would be kept until it was time for the ceremony.

Samonios arrived and the New Year festivities were in full swing. Shortly before midnight Blyth and Gwenn slipped away from the revelry and took the captured wolf to the same place where Teague and Abbon had made their first transformations a year earlier. The moonless night was absolutely clear, and once they were away from the light of the camp fires the only light was from the stars, which seemed to burn holes in the black fabric of the sky. Blyth looked up at the stars and picked out the Gods as they watched down over them. The horse goddess Epona seemed, perhaps, to smile down on him. He remembered watching his mother Epona disappearing over the hills with his little sister Elarch, she on her pony, and his mother leading the packhorse. And then when he saw them again further along, as they crested the next hill, there were three horses, and no sign of his mother. The third horse had a long flowing mane of exactly the same coloured hair as his mother had, and at last he understood.

Their eyes were now as accustomed to the scarce light as they were ever going to be. Blyth could just make out the shape of the sack with the docile wolf inside. Gwenn determined that now was close to midnight, and she turned to Blyth, her pale hair like the first frosts forming on the branches of the willow trees, and told him to open the sack. The wolf, subdued by a charm, crawled out and lay down. Blyth steeled himself one last time for the deed which, deep down, he didn't want to do.

"He doesn't die, Blyth," said Gwenn, sensing his hesitation. "His soul lives on in you."

With a swift and sure movement, Blyth drew the sharp blade across the neck of the wolf and blood spurted over his hands and the forest floor, glistening dimly in the starlight.

Quickly, Gwenn took the knife and cut out the heart, the liver and the brain and cut off a piece of each which Blyth had to eat. Then she spoke the incantations that she had spoken for Abbon and Teague.

"I don't feel any different," said Blyth.

"Start to think like a wolf," Gwenn replied.

And Blyth did so, sniffing the air, he went down on his hands and knees, he arched his back and as he did so, his shape changed, he felt his hind legs shorten, the feet growing longer, slimmer, his toes growing claws and hard pads. He felt his front legs grow stronger, the fingers replaced by paws. Dark shapes were now outlined more clearly as his eyes changed to the amber eyes of a twilight hunter. His ears pricked up as he caught new sounds that were previously unknown to him - the rustle of small rodents in holes, and birds in trees, and much more besides, but his nose was the biggest surprise. He sensed smells that, before, had eluded him, as hard as he had sniffed. Each smell had its own distinct meaning, yet to be unravelled. He wanted to sniff every tree and root, every stone and stream. He snuffled among leaves and moss trying to work out what each smell might mean. His tail wagged, unbidden, as he tasted the air and rejoiced in the power and the freedom of this new shape.

He lifted up his head and howled a rapturous song to the unseen moon, to the stars, to all the Gods and Goddesses in the stars, to the great white backbone of the sky, and to the trees standing around.

Gwenn stood silently framed against the stars, her white hair flowing in the gentle night breeze, clearer now than it was for his weak human eyes.

As the festivities continued in the village of Entwalen-Dun, the sound of revelry and merriment was broken briefly by the plaintive howl of a lone wolf close by. Nobody was worried, although the howl was closer than usual; the villagers continued with their party. But two boys looked at each other and smiled. They quietly slipped away from the feast and headed towards the clearing. As soon as they were clear of the gates, they transformed into a tiger - sleek and powerful, its orange and black stripes almost the same hue in the weak starlight - and a chimpanzee, black and furry, with an intelligent pink face and gentle yet strong hands. The chimpanzee clambered into the trees at the earliest opportunity and surged along the branches in the direction of the howling. The tiger bounded along below him, reaching the clearing first. He slowed as he saw Gwenn standing with the dark grey wolf, and transformed back into Teague, as the chimp landed softly on the forest floor almost instantly turning back

215

into Abbon. The wolf transformed into Blyth and the three brothers met in the middle of the clearing in one big hug as Gwenn watched, smiling, and thought about the future. Before she slept that night she wrote at length on her wax tablet in the strange script of the Deru-Weidi.

25

The morning was bright and crisp; the sky was a brilliant blue, but the grass around the hillside was white with frost. Most of the village slept; even Teague was slow to wake up on this morning. Kaito was the first to stir, feeding the horses and making sure they were warm enough, then bringing the fire to life with a nonchalant wave of his staff, before setting water to boil for morning tea. In fact Bellenos was already quite advanced in his journey before the rest of the group arose. Unusually, Blyth awoke before Teague, and gratefully accepted Kaito's brew. They played a little of the war game before Teague woke and took over from Blyth, who was losing. It wasn't long before Teague had turned the game around and won it, despite not having his Mage.

While they were playing Gwenn woke up and took Blyth outside for a private conversation.

She led the way out of the village gates towards the north. Turning to him, she said, "Your father saw your future before you were even born. Your fate is tied up with a boy the same age as you, born on the same day. He is, in some way, connected with wolves."

"When we were in Rome, I met a boy. He was born on or about the same day as me. I don't think he had any connection with wolves though."

Gwenn looked thoughtful. Then she said, "The Romani have a story that their city was founded by a man called Romulus. He was one of twin boys, Romulus and Remus, who were the rightful heirs to a kingdom, but they were thrown into a river by their uncle. Somehow they survived, and here is the important part, they survived because a she-wolf suckled them. Later they planned to found a new city but they argued, and Romulus killed his brother before founding the city of Rome. So in a sense, every ancient Romani family has wolves to thank for their ancestry."

"So do you think he is the one? He said his name was Gaius Yulius Kaiser, and he was the head of his household, the 'paterfamilias' because his father is dead."

Gwenn looked thoughtful. "I don't know. Perhaps he could be. It is only a matter of time before the Romani find a great war leader who will try to expand their borders again. Whoever it is, we must be ready."

The conversation fell silent now and they stood there, both lost in thought. They were standing on a ridge overlooking the road that approached the village of Entwalen-Dun from the north-west. The sun was warming the ground and melting the frost now; the dewy grass sparkled emerald green. Gwenn appeared intent on the furthest point on the road, and as Blyth followed her gaze he could see horses, still tiny dots in the distance.

"Someone's coming along the road," observed Blyth, conversationally.

"Yes," agreed Gwenn, since no further comment seemed possible at this point.

"Have you thought much of home recently?" she asked Blyth after a little while.

"I don't think I have a home. I miss my mother but I'm a man now and I suppose, like Gaius, I am the 'paterfamilias' now."

He thought briefly also of Blodwyth, but decided not to mention that.

As they drew closer, Blyth could see three horses with one rider. There was a pale white pony with a rider, another was loaded with saddle bags, and the third was bare-backed. It had a long flowing mane of reddish gold. Blyth remembered again, seeing three horses and one rider disappearing over the crest of a hill and he wondered.

"Yes Blyth," Gwenn said, to his unuttered question. She was watching his face. It was as though she could read his thoughts.

Blyth broke into a grin, and then started running

along the path towards the three horses. The horses in their turn broke into a canter, and then as they came closer, the larger of the two transformed in mid bound into Blyth's mother Epona, who swept him up in a crushing hug. As soon as his mother released him, his sister Elarch dismounted like a gymnast from her pony and almost flew into his arms. It was over three years since he had seen her. Yes, he was taller now, taller than his mother but Elarch had seemingly shot up, and she was no longer sickly. Her hair was still platinum blonde, but her skin was not pale and her eyes and smile were brighter than the sun. She wore several delicate torcs on her long neck, and a flowing white tunic with loose sleeves that hung from her outstretched arms. Her laugh was like falling water, and although she was still slim, and as light as a feather, she could hug like a bear.

Gwenn waited patiently for the little family reunion, and then Epona embraced her like a sister. They walked the rest of the way to the village. Elarch could not stop talking to Blyth, who half listened to her babbling as it broke over him like waves on a boat. Gwenn and Epona walked along behind in silence, as though they had exchanged all the information they needed to already, which of course they had.

The group arrived back at the fort and headed for the roundhouse where Kaito, Abbon, and Teague were. Teague had his back to the doorway and was intent on the war game which he was playing alone, trying to practise in the absence of a real opponent. Kaito was busying himself with making a rich, warming stew. So it was Abbon, who was idly trying to kill a fly with a swatter woven from grass and reeds, who saw them first.

"Mother!" he shouted, as he jumped to give her a hug. Teague spun round half expecting it to be a joke, and then saw Abbon in a group hug with Epona and Elarch. He joined in briefly although, as a man himself now, he felt that he could not show as much excitement as his little brother. Kaito had poured out tea for everyone and handed out cups now.

"You must be tired," he said, and he indicated seats covered with furs for them to sit.

The whole family had so many stories to relate, nobody knew quite where to begin. They interrupted each other constantly with anecdotes and observations that related to their own tales, but gradually each thread of the story was unwoven and rewoven into a more complete fabric. Epona had spent time with the Eceni Mawr, Catuvellauni, Trinovantes, Belgae, Atrebates, and the Cantiaci. The tribes of Pretan were no more united than they had been before the boys had left their home village; but they were at least aware of the possible threat from the Romani. Some Chiefs agreed that, if the Romani did attack Gaul, it would be fun to join with the Galli in defeating them. Perhaps there would be spoils, and even a chance to attack Rome itself, just like the hero Brynno. A few were persuaded that the Romani presented a real threat and that it would take a united effort to repulse them; these were mainly those who were already being advised by Deru-Weidi in their tribe. Many simply could not believe that the Romani represented a real threat. It was said that they were involved in a civil war with two powerful generals fighting each other for control, and most of the fighting was to the south and east. Gaul was not even important to them. Urien certainly was not interested, despite the efforts of Golow-Vur, the enmity between Urien and Trethiwr's sons now being irrevocable. The further away from Gaul, the more the tribes felt that while Rome might well be a threat, it would not stand a chance against their invincible warriors. The Silures, Ordovices, and Brigantes were especially confident, although Epona knew they were not as invincible as they thought themselves.

Epona was open to the idea that this Gaius Yulius Kaiser could well be the man who Trethiwr had dreamed of, the man born on the same day as Blyth, and of a city that owed its very existence to wolves.

"We need someone to keep track of him," she said.

"I will see to it," said Gwenn immediately. "These boys still have training to attend to. They are not ready to be Deru-Weidi yet, as our recent adventures have proved."

"What?" began Blyth, but his mother shushed him and said, "It takes 20 years to train as a Deru-Weido, you have spent just a few years of greatly interrupted training and even as natural as you are, there is much more you must learn."

"We are banned from the oak groves at Lugh-Dun," announced Blyth, with a mixture of pride and finality.

"Which is why you are going to Ynis-Mona to finish your studies."

"But… " began Blyth, but his mother was stone faced and stopped him with a look, and the hunting gesture for silence.

The next day the whole family, Kaito, Epona, the boys and Elarch, departed on horseback heading north through the territory of the Lingones and beyond, to the port of the Morini, where they could take a short sea voyage to the lands of the Cantiaci. It was dangerous travelling in winter, but both Gwenn and Epona were adamant that they should not delay. They waved goodbye to Gwenn, who was herself leaving in the opposite direction to make plans to locate and watch Gaius Yulius Kaiser.

It would be many moons before the boys reached their destination in the far north of the lands of the Ordovices, and many years of training lay before them. Blyth hoped it would all be worth the effort in the end. Frost lay all around once more and nobody had much to say as they rode along the path, leaving the fortress of Entwalen-Dun behind them.

Gwenn's thoughts wandered to the preparation for her next task. She decided there was a new power she would need to master before returning to Rome.

Notes.

This is a fictional story based in a real world; a world which is only partly understood by historians. The Celtic people of Europe, before the Roman conquest, did not write much down. Although they must have had knowledge of writing, they preferred to memorise stories and information. As a result, what little we know is pieced together from archaeological evidence and the writings of Roman and Greek historians.

Much of what we think we know is biased because it is written by the ultimate victors in the long struggle for supremacy between Celts and Romans. For example, the story of Brennus sacking Rome in 400BC is told by Roman historians, writing long after the event, with the natural bias in favour of their own people. I am certain that the Celtic bards or Druids would have told the story differently, and I attempt to envisage such a story in the text of this book.

Sometimes, Roman writers may have got things wrong because they simply did not fully understand Celtic ways. Descriptions of wicker baskets full of human sacrifices may well have been a fabrication, or at least an exaggeration. Meanwhile, the Romans also had barbaric rituals including crucifixion, setting wild animals upon those convicted of dubious crimes, and of course allowing men to fight each other to the death.

Life in those times, indeed throughout most of human history from the first civilisations to the present day, was brutal. Human life was cheap, especially if it was the life of an enemy. The pre-Roman Celts (I am given to understand) believed fervently in an afterlife: much like the later Christian view of Heaven. Death held no fear for them, and courage in battle was highly prized. But unlike the Romans, who also prized military prowess, they had little or no loyalty beyond that which they gave to their local chief.

I make no pretence that the Celts were perfect, and the Romans all bad. However, one could debate that the world may well have been a slightly better place if the Celts had won. They were, broadly speaking, more artistic and individualistic than the Romans, prizing music, poetry and crafts as highly as warfare. They were also far more egalitarian, allowing women to adopt what the Romano-Greek culture saw as purely male roles including being the tribal leader, entering the priesthood, and even fighting as warriors. They were of course highly religious, worshipping many Gods and Goddesses, with many of the concepts that made adopting Christianity very easy for them. What they did not have was a very strong sense of nationality; tribes were independent of each other.

The Celts also, almost certainly, kept slaves, although not on the same industrial scale that the Romans did. When we imagine Celtic life we visualise warriors based in a hill-fort overlooking the landscape. That landscape was full of farms growing a variety of crops and rearing cattle, sheep, pigs and chickens. Warriors did not work on farms; they were supplied with food in exchange for protection from bandits and invading warriors from other tribes. The farmers had little or no security and had no option but to provide the warriors with food.

I have tried to stick as closely as possible to real history as far as we know it, although I have allowed myself to assume a few things for which there is, at best, circumstantial evidence. For example, woven drapes inside roundhouses for insulation and decoration, the idea of houses painted with bright colours, and in particular the 'war game' played by the boys on a board with little pieces that closely resemble those of a chess set.

The magic used in the story varies from the perfectly believable, to the downright fantastic. Psychological trickery is real enough; curses can be incredibly powerful if the person cursed really believes in the power of the magician. Science is also used, from smokescreens that rely on chemistry, to drinks that give a person special powers. Today, coffee and tea used as stimulants, and other drugs help with sleep. There are also chemicals which will render a person far stronger than normal and prevent them from feeling pain. The magic potion of Asterix and Obelix is not completely without a real life equivalent, albeit the user was, in no way, rendered invulnerable.

Some of the ingredients for Druid potions would have grown locally, but I have made a fairly huge leap in asserting that certain Celts, with specialist knowledge, also obtained ingredients from traders who travelled further afield: to both the Americas, and to the Far East. Although there is not one single scrap of hard evidence to support this, there is a certain amount of circumstantial evidence and I have chosen to accept this as enough reason to allow it in a work of fiction.

I am not, however, aware of any scientific theory that permits a human to transform into an animal, but the Celtic myths of such transformations make it an essential ingredient in any such story.

Lastly, the reason why none of the magical events in

this story, or the existence of dragons, ever became part of written history is because the Deru-Weidi (Druids) were so secretive that they swore never to reveal their powers to outsiders. In the story, they cannot openly use magic, even in self-defence. In a tight spot, the Druid would simply accept death rather than show the Romans their secret arts. After all, Lugh would be waiting for them in the next world.

The Celts believed that the world began with darkness and then light was created. Therefore each day began at sunset, and each year began with the onset of winter; Samonios (Halloween) being the New Year. They had numbers but rarely had a need to talk of very large numbers specifically, therefore sometimes you will see phrases like fifty times fifty, or ten-hundred. I have tried to write as much as possible using terms and metaphors that could have made sense to a Celt, but of course, I am using imagination and guesswork about most of this. My main aim was to avoid assuming that the reader needs everything to be explained to them.

PRONUNCIATION

Some of the Celtic names in the book are made up from proto-Celtic or existing languages like Welsh and Breton. Others are actual names. Nobody really knows exactly how the Iron-age Celts spoke, but I have assumed a similarity to Welsh. In my mind, 'R' is usually rolled as in Italian, but if you have trouble with that don't worry. In fact, please pronounce any name as you wish and if anyone tells you it's wrong, point to this sentence.

- Blodwyth – Blod-uith
- Blyth – Rhymes with scythe
- Cuilleana – Quill-e-aa-na
- Darruwen – Long 'a'
- Durgal – Long 'u' rolled 'r'
- Elarch – Ell-ark - roll the 'r', 'ch' as in 'loch'
- Kaito – Kay-toe
- Kyndyrn – Kin-d'yi-rn
- Ruthgem – Roll the 'r' – the 'g' is not soft like the English 'gem' nor hard like 'get' it is more in the back of the throat like a cross between 'g' and 'h' *I'm really sorry, even I don't know why, but it is.*
- Teague – Teeg
- Trethiwr – Treth-yewerr (hard 'th')
- Urien – You-rr-i-en

GLOSSARY

A few terms in the text may not make sense immediately. So here's a handy guide to some of the more obscure names.

Gods and historical characters

- Bellenos – sun god, equivalent to Apollo.
- Brynno – my imagined Celtic spelling of Brennus.
- Brigantia – Brighid or Bride, the Celtic goddess who releases spring from the grip of winter.
- Cernunnos – a horned god.
- Govanno – a god of alcohol.
- Poeninos – god of a specific mountain in the Alps.
- Leucretios – a god of lightning.
- Taranis – a god of thunder.
- Lenus – a god of healing.
- Deus Pater – also spelled Dis-Fater when pronounced by the Germanic Celts of Entwalen-Dun (equivalent to Jupiter/Zeus).

Places and tribes

- Armorica – an area equivalent to modern day Brittany.
- Ba-dun – a hill fort not far from modern day Dorchester.
- Bibracte – Gaulish town.
- Boii - a Celtic tribe.
- Carnuti – a Gaulish tribe.
- Catuvellauni, Trinovantes, Belgae, Atrebates, and the Cantiaci – some Celtic tribes of Britain.
- Cosedia – a port in northern Gaul, now modern day Coutances in Normandy.
- Dumnoreix – a Gaulish chieftain.
- Dwr-y-tryges – tribal name for the people who lived in Dorset and parts of Somerset.
- Eceni Mawr – the Iceni (hard 'c').
- Eiru – Ireland.
- Entwalen-Dun – hill-fort between two lakes.
- Eryri – Eagle people (fictional name of a tribe from a mythical era in the distant past).
- Genabo – a Gaulish town, Cenabum in Latin, equivalent to modern day Orléans.
- Helleni – Greeks.
- Keltoi – the Greek name for all the Celtic peoples.
- Lingones and Morini – Gaulish tribes around modern Belgium.

- Lugh-Dun – Lugdunum, another Gaulish town. Modern-day Lyons.
- Massalia – modern day Marseilles. Founded by Greeks but under Roman protection/control by the period of the story.
- Maywr-dun – a larger hillfort. Maywr means big or great.
- Narbo – Roman garrison town - modern day Narbonne.
- Nevez-Dun – a Gaulish town. The name is back- imagined from the Latin Noviodunum.
- Pretan – the island we now call Britain.
- Pretani – the people of Pretan - a general term and not a tribal name.
- Roma – Rome.
- Romani – Romans.
- Sennoni – a Celtic tribe usually written as the Senones.
- Silures and Ordovici – Celtic tribes of Wales.
- Suindinum - chief town of the Cenomanni - modern day Le Mans.
- Unelli – Gaulish tribe in modern day Normandy.
- Unellia – land of the Unelli.
- Ynis-Mona – Anglesey (modern day Ynis Mon in Welsh).
- Y-Trwsgani – an imagined Celtic rendering of Etruscans.

Other

- Belotonios - Beltane, the start of summer and the second most important festival in the Celtic year after Samhain. The Celts celebrated the cross quarter festivals, between the solstices and equinoxes. Theirs was emphatically a lunar calendar and it is likely that feasts were held at a significant point on the lunar cycle, not on a fixed date in the solar year. In other words, much more like Easter than May Day.

- Brachii – trousers. The Celts appear to have invented trousers, instead of wearing tunics and togas as the Romans and Greeks did.

- Contubernium – a small unit of Roman soldiers consisting of eight legionaries and two supporting servants.

- Decanus – leader of the ten men in the contubernium.

- Deru-Weidi – Druids - the name is a back creation based on an ancient word for the oak tree, 'Deru', and the root of our modern word Wise, 'Weido/i'.

- Deru-Weido – a Druid.

- Imbolc – the end of winter when the ewes start to come into milk and lambing season begins. Around the end of February.

- Lugunasath – Lughnasadh – the end of summer. Harvest time.
- Retiarius – a type of gladiator who used a fishing net and trident
- Riurios – a month according to the Coligny calendar, approximately equivalent to December.
- Samonios – Samhain (pronounced 'Sow-een') – the origin of our modern Halloween festival and the Celtic New Year. The most important feast in the Celtic year, when the veil between this world and the next is thinnest, allowing for the possibility of communication with the dead.
- Thermopolia – (singular Thermopolium) a kind of café, not to be confused with Thermopylae, the famous battle.

ABOUT THE AUTHOR

Oliver was born in London and went to Colfe's School in Lee where, despite the efforts of numerous highly respected teachers, he scraped a handful of O' levels and drifted into a random series of jobs.

Having become a father, he began working on his family tree, which led to a website about his grandfather, the writer and explorer Frank Kingdon-Ward. This in turn led to his first paid writing job, a 1,200 word article on Kingdon-Ward for a book; 'The Great Explorers' by Robin Hanbury-Tenison (Thames and Hudson ISBN13: 9780500251690)

He has also written a series of books for younger readers, the 'Time Tunnel' series, under the author name Olli Tooley.

Oliver now lives in North Devon with his wife and four children, and spends his time writing, presenting a local radio show featuring unsigned musicians, shouting at people to get ready for school, and arguing with people on social media.

PREVIEW OF BOOK 2
WOMEN OF THE WISE OAK

1

Gwenn's breath froze on the fur round her hood. If she wasn't freezing cold, and clinging on to a sliver of ice-coated rock, she might have enjoyed the play of moonlight on the tiny ice crystals. Painfully, gasping for air, she pulled her leg up, bit by bit, until it reached the foothold beside her elbow. She pushed down against it. One last effort and she would be able to rest. Her hand found a hold that didn't give way, and with a huge mental effort, calling on her last reserves of strength, she managed to swing one leg over the top and rolled breathless, aching with cold, onto the narrow flat ledge. She was halfway up the mountain on a steep face, crusted with ice, with pockets of snow here and there, still unmelted from the previous winter. Dotted along the ledge, and on others above and below her, there were large nests of sticks woven in crazy piles, as if a storm had tried to build a roundhouse. From the nearest, a dozen paces away, a huge brown bird eyed her suspiciously as it tried to conceal the three fledgling chicks in the nest. Tiny plants fought to squeeze into the smallest crevices in the rock face, some with fat hairy leaves, others with waxy leaves, or miniscule flowers in purples, blues and yellows.

Without her magic Gwenn would be dead by sunrise: even with it she would struggle. She pulled her staff from the pack on her back and pointed it at the bare rock. A fire sprang up out of nothing, crackling with an orange flame, tinged with green. It took almost the last of her energy to do that, so her next thought was food. She pulled off her thin leather mittens and struggled at the ties of her pack with numbed fingers. The cold was deep in her bones; she could feel it biting at her fingers. She would need something hot inside her, and soon. Gwenn preferred not to eat meat. She had prepared a mixture of ground oats, nuts, and honey; formed into small cakes. She ate some now. She had brought some wood, which she now added to the fire, as it could not be expected to burn indefinitely on magic alone. Then she set water to warm for tea. Once the water had boiled, and the tea infused, she drank it in small short sips, as quickly as she could bear, cupping her hands around the vessel to warm them.

As the hot liquid and high energy food took effect

she was able to relax a little more. Bellenos was long gone on his journey through the dark realms. A black lake below reflected the almost full moon in its depths. Gwenn wrote on her wax tablet. She could write the strange straight lines of Deru-Weidi script in complete darkness if she had to. Then she pulled her furs around her and slept, close to the fire.

Gwenn dreamed of falling; the fall went on seemingly forever, until she woke with a start. The moon was gone now and it was bitterly cold. The only light was from the stars and the little fire which had burned down to embers. Gwenn fed it some more firewood and set the remains of her tea to warm on it, toasting the little cakes while she waited. She gulped the hot liquid down as soon as it was ready, and burned her mouth on the cakes as she ate. With mittens still on, she toasted her hands and feet over the flames and tucked the hot mittens inside her outer garment.

Before sleep could return the stars were fading. The dome of inky black faded gradually to woad, and then to a milky white on the horizon, before Bellenos made his grand entrance. Gwenn closed her eyelids just enough to continue looking straight at the rising sun trying to make out the form of the God who, according to legend, rode his fiery chariot across the sky every day. She gazed at the disc of searing light and wondered for the first time if the story might not be the whole truth.

The eagles were stirring in the nest, the adult birds unwilling to depart while there was a human so close by.

Squeaking pathetically at Gwenn, their call belied their awesome appearance. Gwenn stood and stamped some life into her frozen feet. The eagles reared and spread their wings in a threatening display.

There was not a single cloud in the sky today and, although the air was still freezing cold at this altitude, Gwenn could feel the warmth flowing into her as she stood facing the sun. The fire was dying down now she fed it the last of her wood. She was down to one last water skin and some dried fungi.

As the day wore on, the fledglings began to test their wings, stretching and catching the updraughts. First one, then another, took off from the ledge and half flew, half tumbled, to a lower ledge. They returned, as clumsily as they left, to the nest where the third chick was still unprepared for this next adventure. It was clearly smaller than the other two. The adult birds stood guard, wary of Gwenn's presence, but eventually they would have to fly off in search of food. Gwenn waited as though her life depended on patience. It did. With limited food and water; if she failed in her goal, if her resolve left her, she would almost certainly die on the descent from the mountain.

With the increasing squeaks of demanding and hungry eaglets, one of the adults took off in search of food. It soared over the warm air rushing up the cliff face, driven by the heat of the sun on the fields far below. It was a mere speck in the distance before the older two chicks had another experimental flight. The runt of the clutch remained in the nest as the other two returned, this time with more assurance. Eventually the second adult took wing and stooped a short way, gathering speed before soaring gracefully off over the green and gold landscape.

Gwenn stiffened her resolve. This would most likely be her only chance. As she inched along the ledge, she watched the older two eaglets turn on their weaker sibling. With a few vicious stabs they killed it, and then tore it apart and ate it. That was the turning point in her internal battle. To kill one of these majestic creatures and absorb its life and soul was not an action she could take lightly, but seeing the savage way they killed their own kin made the next deed much easier to bear.

She pointed her staff at the two remaining birds. They went still and silent, surrounded by a shimmering haze in the air. Inching along the ledge, which got narrower the closer she got, she was able to drop a leather bag over one of the remaining birds and lift it clear of the nest. In the darkness of the sack, the fledgling remained motionless.

Now Gwenn inched back to the wider part of the ledge, and then climbed a little higher to another ledge which was out of sight of the nest.

She basked in the warming rays of the sun and her stomach rumbled. She ate the dried fungi. She should have soaked them first. They were chewy and tasteless. She drank a mouthful of water, and continued her vigil, waiting patiently for the sun to set and the full moon to rise. Time had never moved so slowly for Gwenn. But she had reserves of patience born of necessity, and she sat stoically until the sun finally began to set. Clouds had gathered in the valleys below her. A cirque lake just above the level of the mists glimmered under faint wisps of stray mist like a rich warming stew bubbling over the fire. Clouds covered all the land below the tree line and it felt to Gwenn as though she was in the next world, and her village far below was still in the world of the living. If her plan failed then that feeling would soon become reality.

The horizon caught fire, glowing a thousand shades of orange. She saw one eagle parent return: the female, Gwenn deduced, as it was the larger of the two. She drank the last of her water, and waited still. Moonlight played on the crystals of ice on the rocks. Gwenn's breath once more turned to clouds and tiny droplets began to freeze once more. Still she waited.

When she deduced it was nearly midnight, she carefully opened the sack containing the unfortunate fledgling eagle. It flapped before the sack was even fully open and a sharp beak darted out, slashing through her mitten and lacerating her hand. She just about managed to get her other hand around the back of its neck and grip tightly while it flapped its wings, almost knocking them both off the ledge. For all the time she had spent studying these majestic creatures, she had never imagined that a young one could put up such a fierce fight. With her bleeding hand glistening in the moonlight she slashed a flint knife across the bird's throat and the eagle's blood mingled with her own, running down her hand and onto the frosty ledge.

Now the bird lay limp in her hands she quickly cut it open and extracted the parts she needed for the ceremony: the brain, liver, and heart. She cut off a piece of each and ate them raw, reciting secret words taught to her decades before. Still she waited, hungry, cold, tired and now bleeding profusely. She tore a strip of material from her tunic and tied it round the wound. She recalled her dream from the previous night: falling, falling for ever, with no sight of the ground, just a dream-borne mist below her, and the eternal falling. She had not slept, she felt dizzy, she felt like she was really falling. There was a faint buzzing sound inside her head, and then she passed out.

Gwenn awoke with the first rays of the morning sun. She assumed she hadn't died because her hand still hurt. Another multi-coloured display of nature's extravagant artistic style emblazoned the eastern sky. This was it; there was no going back, and no more waiting. She stood on the ledge, and faced the drop before her. This was not a dream; she looked down at the very real mist below her and wondered how long she could fall before she hit the rocks beneath the mists. Would she hit them at all? Would she instead just keep falling through eternal mists? Would she feel the pain of smashing into the rocks? Would death be instant? Would she fall until she emerged in the next world, to be greeted in the halls of Lugh?

There really was only one way to find out, and she would rather die quickly than starve to death or die of cold trying to climb down the mountain. She stood on the ledge and faced the abyss. Hands outstretched, she allowed herself to fall forward and then, with a push from her legs, she plummeted head first down the cliff face.